Sand
and
Other
Flash
Fiction

Also by Michael Scofield from Sunstone Press

Acting Badly

Making Crazy

Smut Busters

Whirling Backward into the World

Circus Americana and Other Poems

Dedicated Lives: Talks with those Helping Others

Sand
and
Other
Flash
Fiction

Michael Scofield

SUNSTONE PRESS

SANTA FE

This book is a work of fiction. Names, characters, places, and incidents are either the product of the author's imagination or are used fictitiously.

Sunstone books may be purchased for educational, business, or sales promotional use. For information please write: Special Markets Department, Sunstone Press, P.O. Box 2321, Santa Fe, New Mexico 87504-2321.

Book and cover design › Vicki Ahl
Body typeface › Californian FB
Printed on acid-free paper
∞
eBook 978-1-61139-382-8

Library of Congress Cataloging-in-Publication Data

Scofield, Michael.
[Short stories. Selections]
Sand and other flash fiction / by Michael Scofield.
    pages ; cm
ISBN 978-1-63293-066-8 (softcover : alk. paper)
I. Title.
PS3619.C63A6 2015
813'.6--dc23

2015013517

WWW.SUNSTONEPRESS.COM
SUNSTONE PRESS / POST OFFICE BOX 2321 / SANTA FE, NM 87504-2321 /USA
(505) 988-4418 / ORDERS ONLY (800) 243-5644 / FAX (505) 988-1025

for Noreen

Acknowledgments

I'm grateful to the following friends who shared true incidents upon which some of these snippets are based: Stephanie Burns, Eliot Kohen, Richard Lehnert, Dana Levin, Chip Lilianthal, Noreen Norris, Rick Remington, Barbara Rockman, Mary Ellen Scofield, Marian Shirin, Karen Squires, Mary Stein, John Valdes, G. Sterling Zinsmeyer.

Thanks to Matt Roybal for his help in formatting my original manuscript.

Contents

Preface

"I don't know what I'd do without you, Gin."

"Let's find out."

"Find out?"

"What you'll do. I'm leaving for two weeks."

So begins "Exhaustion," one of the sixty-eight flash fictions in this book, conceived as prompts for scriptwriters looking for movie ideas, and as stand-alone, very short stories.

The common definition of flash fiction is a story of less than 1,000 words that emphasizes plot and has a beginning, middle, and often a surprise ending. The technique has accumulated many nicknames: short-short, sudden fiction, furious fiction, postcard fiction, nanofiction, microstories.

Very short fiction goes back as far as *Aesop's Fables*. Well-known practitioners in English include Lydia Davis, Sam Shepard, Ray Bradbury, Kurt Vonnegut, Ernest Hemingway, even the composer, John Cage.

My own brand of flash fiction sometimes varies from tradition. "Sloppy," for instance, starts this way:

Financially, Jacques had no need. He owned his Porche outright, purchased vests from Pendleton. So why shoplift?

And here's how "Sloppy" tapers off: "Had he made the smooth move, he wondered?" No surprise ending, nor a closing—more an opening meant to result in a feature film or to spur your imagination as reader to come up with more obstacles for Jacques, more plot twists, perhaps a devoted (or double-crossing) companion in crime.

Flash fiction has become popular with those of us craving a rush but having scant time to read. Thus the annual *World's Best Short-Short Story Contest* out of Florida State University, the anthologies *New Sudden Fiction* and *Flash Fiction Forward*, the zine *Flash Fiction Online*. For vexed souls who have zero time to read stories, National Public Radio broadcasts winners of its *Three Minute Fiction* contest.

You'll find in my collection a one-sentence summary—called a 'log line' in the TV and movie trades—capping each story. The log line for "Reality Check," for instance, reads, "When Miles at age forty-one leaves his barren wife for someone who can give him children, the candidate he chooses harbors a discouraging secret." These summaries are designed to help you pick the 400-to-900-word stories that probably are going to fit your mood best.

Thanks for buying this book. I'm betting you'll enjoy some of the unexpected story lines—at the least you'll meet a lot of intriguing characters, not a few of whom you may feel you know well.

—Michael Scofield
Santa Fe

First Date

Late-septuagenarians Martin and Bridget hope to find a little fun during lunch at the Purple Mesa but never expect that fun to come from a mix-up in pills.

"What can I get you two?" The blonde flipped her ponytail up.

Martin and Bridget, approaching eighty and long bereft of spouses, had become acquainted as ushers during the annual series of Lannan lectures. Three more months had to pass before Martin found the courage to ask Bridget out.

He'd chosen the Purple Mesa Eatery for its linen, spread on tables spaced a courteous distance apart. For today's lunch Bridget wore a flowered jacket, white blouse, and crushed-cotton skirt. Martin supposed his hearing aids could not be much of a turn-on, and found her scarlet mop of hair silly, but she kept her weight down and he'd grown partial to her throaty harmonics.

"More time?" the waitress asked.

"No, no. Martin, are you ready?"

"Sure am," he said, sitting kitty-corner to her. His left hand started shaking. It knuckled the box of pills in his pocket as he hid the hand under his butt.

"For me," Bridget said, "a cup of the broccoli soup and half a portobello sandwich."

"To drink?"

"Water's fine. No ice."

"And you, sir?"

"Same."

After the waitress had brought their waters, Martin lifted his hip. "You'll have to excuse me." He placed the blue box sectioned into compartments, *Morn, Noon, Din,* and *Eve,* on the creased tablecloth. "A nuisance but they keep me out of trouble." He thumbed open the polypropylene top of *Noon* and dumped out half a dozen pills.

"Well, Martin, thanks for the lead." Bridget unsnapped the embroidered purse she'd hung from her chair and produced a leather pouch. She loosened the drawstring and upended it. A dozen caplets, tablets—some halved—blue-and-white capsules, and adobe-colored gels poured forth.

"My gosh!"

"The years have taken their toll," she said. "Too many good times, I'm afraid."

"Laugh for me again, will you?"

"Well, sure. About what?"

"How we're trying to find a little fun in the face of all this." He flung out his left arm to indicate the medicinal array. His fingers missed her glass but the heel of his hand swept most of the pills across the carpeting's woven mesas.

"Oh, Martin!"

He stood as the blonde carried in their lunches. "I screwed up," he told her. "Sinking to my knees may take a little time. Rising will take a lot more."

"Sir, please, stay." The girl set the tray on the table and, laughing, clapped her chest. "I'm sorry." She crouched. "Who gets what?"

"The two tabs that look too large to swallow are mine," Bridget said. "And the three halves with sharp corners requiring several gulps. Isn't this too awful?"

By now Martin was laughing, too. "Can you believe we're so needy?"

Bridget's scarlet mop tossed as she shook her head.

"That sky-blue gel is mine," Martin said. "So is the lozenge that keeps my heart pumping. And the two tiny whites."

"I've got a lozenge down there for dizzy spells."

"Which of the rest is whose?"

Martin looked at Bridget and threw up his hands. She shrugged.

"How about this?" asked the waitress. "I give you the ones we know and then we just divvy up?"

The family of four nearby and another couple had also started laughing.

"Oh, my, Martin," said Bridget, "I think we've found our fun. Shall we drink some bubbly, I mean Alka-Seltzer, to toast a lovely lunch?"

Too Many Options

Though Caitlin, enjoying an affair with Florian, has invited him for dinner with her daughters and bisexual husband, Florian isn't sure he has the stomach for it.

The set of tennis with Caitlin in the park near Florian's one-bedroom had felt real enough: asphalt, two rackets, yellow lines, slack net, new can of balls.

His present actions did not: belly slapping hers, groanings, her scream, his collapse.

He rolled off and kissed her eyelids and slight breasts while her fingers set off those happy aftershocks she no longer sought at home.

When she stopped panting, he asked, "Do you really think you can do this dinner tonight?"

"Dessert's done. Shauna's watching the roast. I can if *you're* up for it."

"If I'm up, there's no way."

They laughed and embraced and watched a junco swoop to the birdbath he kept filled in his patio.

"Darling," Caitlin said, "a month earlier I would have left him, I swear it."

"You've told me."

"But he's given up balling his boy toy at the bank and—"

"How do you know that?"

"I believe him is all. And he and I've got the girls. You don't want to add them to your two, right?"

"I guess."

"It's an impossible situation, Florian."

"Except that I've fallen for you."

"We can keep meeting."

"Tennis, anyone?"

"Stop it. Not *anyone*." She kissed his earlobe.

▲▲▲

A couple of hours later he found himself at one end of the Roberts' dining table. Caitlin's husband, Rick—dressed in polo, khakis, and loafers without socks—sat at the table's far end. Caitlin sat next to her younger daughter, Sam for Samantha, and Shauna sat in short-shorts opposite.

The table's centerpiece held the pot roast's remains, surrounded by scraps of carrots and potatoes. Nearby soared the daylilies Florian had brought to this low-slung adobe with its three gardens that Caitlin and the girls kept trim. He had recently written up and photographed the landscaping for a free-lance assignment from *Sunset Magazine*.

"Good, Cait." Rick patted his paunch. "Girls?"

"What?" asked Shauna.

"Mom cooked a dish we don't often have. You liked it?"

"Sure."

"I loved it," Sam said.

"Delicious," added Florian, wondering if he could check his growing nausea until reaching his own bathroom. Was he really staring down the table at a cuckolded, bisexual banker? Maybe Caitlin was doing the right thing, staying. Maybe Florian should call his ex and offer to get into counseling.

"More cabernet, Flor?" Rick asked.

He wagged his head.

Rick emptied the bottle into his glass. "We've got us a special dessert, too, love? My lordy lord, anyone with a name like Florian who scrapes together a living writing about trees and flowers deserves a huge serving of, what's it called again, love?"

"Tiramisu." Caitlin reached for the platter of leftovers and stood.

"I'll help," Florian said, doubting his stomach's steadfastness.

"Stay right there. Shauna, give me a hand."

After clearing away the dishes, Caitlin and Shauna brought out trays holding plates of Madera- and espresso-soaked ladyfingers wedged between layers of whipped eggs, cream, and Mascarpone cheese, each serving drizzled with chocolate.

"Optimum," Rick said after Shauna set down one of the plates embossed with red poppies. "Love, we do thank you." He lifted a forkful of the Tuscan delicacy and closed his eyes. "Oh, my."

On his own first bite, however, Florian jumped up. "The bathroom? Which way?"

Mom

Nine-year-old Jeremy, father dead from a knife wound last year, likes his mom to call him Jock, not honeybunch, especially in front of his Little League teammates.

"Go, man, go; go, man, go; hit it all the way to Pluto; hit it to the North Pole."

So shout the nine-year-old Mudcats, squirming under polypropylene hard hats. They wait on the bench behind a chain link fence that separates the field from four-tiered bleachers.

Braces glinting, Jock, the Mudcats' catcher—hopefully up next—leaps like a fledgling and throws out his scrawny arms. "Good eye, man. Go, man, go."

Jock's father, former manager of Boots & Jackets, was fatally knifed during a break-in last fall. Jock's mother sits on the bleachers' lowest row, a skein of wool and half-finished sweater in her lap. She's gained forty pounds since her husband's death, continues to call her son Jock, as her husband did, though she sometimes slips into honeybunch. The birth certificate reads Jeremy.

"You can do it," growls the Mudcats' coach, belly dangling over his Levis. "Watch the ball all the way in—why are you looking at *me*?"

The Durham Bulls' coach, a scarecrow of a man with a scar crossing his Adam's apple, stands behind the pitching machine. "Wake up out there. How many outs, Bulls?"

"Two," come the cries back.

"How many bases filled?"

"All."

"Looking good. Step and throw. Hustle, guys, hustle, hustle."

He turns toward the Bulls' batter. "A little closer to the plate, buddy. Bring your bat higher. That's right—ready? One. Two." He lowers the pitching machine's arm. "Three."

The softball arcs toward a chubby eight-year-old, who squinches his eyes and swings as though hefting lead instead of aluminum. The bat leaves his grip and spins through the dust toward third.

"It's okay, buddy, don't cry. It's all right."

The Mudcats exchange hard hats for cloth caps as the teams change sides. Jock fits on a catcher's mitt far wider than his face, plants himself behind home, and squats.

"That's it, honeybunch."

"Quit calling me that, Mom."

"Sorry, Jocko."

The Mudcats' big-bellied coach ambles toward the pitching machine as Bulls' batter number one slants the bat above his shoulder.

"Honeybunch!" his mother hisses.

The young catcher twists to face her.

"Keep your fingers pressed tight together in that glove. I don't want one breaking before your violin lesson."

Battling Medicos

When Rhonda's doctor disagrees with the wife he's divorcing (Rhonda's psychiatrist) that Rhonda needs a calming two milligrams of lorazepam, Rhonda can't even leave her chair.

If only her primary care physician and her psychiatrist hadn't been divorcing each other, Rhonda could maybe get the former to ring up the latter and agree to what dosage of lorazepam would best calm her down at night, shy of addiction.

The morning's first patient, Rhonda sat in the physician's office in the soberest outfit she could think to assemble: jacket, blouse, slacks, flats. Her purse holding the psychiatrist's report lay on her lap. To pass time, she practiced her posture: head up, shoulder blades thrown toward each other. Whenever the receptionist left her desk, Rhonda stretched her tongue out and curled it back, using a technique her drunken sister in Spokane had shared for reducing jowls.

Hopefully the lorazepam would stop the tremor in Rhonda's right hand. She smelled her wrist. Enough scent to seem stylish?

Dr. Apel strode into the waiting room in his lab coat, stethoscope swinging. A bearish man with hair brushed back unparted, mustachioed and dimpled, he always looked to Rhonda more woodsman than professional healer. He curled his fingers for her to follow past the lineup of wooden bowls he turned on weekends.

"Get the door, will you?" As usual he plopped on the five-legged stool and threw his hand toward the chair.

"You've read the photocopy I dropped by?" Rhonda asked, hanging her purse from the chair's arm.

"I tried. Madeline could have done us a favor by typing it up."

While Rhonda unfolded the pages of handwriting that had taken her twenty minutes to decode, Dr. Apel started in:

"Madeline has always been given to excess. In this case she's overprescribed. Agreed, we need to do something about your concern that your sister has followed your mother into alcoholism. Need to get you back to a good night's sleep, add some pounds, quiet that hand. Your blood pressure's high, we know that, and I'll have Amy check again before you leave. Half a milligram of lorazepam twice a day—worth trying? Sure. Double that? Can't buy it, Rhonda. Wouldn't dare let you drive."

She turned to the report's second page. "Doctor Apel—"

"Yes?"

"No, your wife, I mean—"

"*Goddamn*, I wish she'd use her maiden name. It's very confusing. Do you think she's actually helping you?"

Rhonda cupped a breast and swallowed. She felt like socking him. But over the past five years he'd prescribed something that had stopped heartburn in its tracks, directed her to a dermatologist who'd known how to wipe out hives, on and on. Had offered what always seemed apt advice.

"I've had too many traumas," Rhonda said.

"Your son's paralysis; watching the train cut the pickup in two—body parts; losing that interior-decorating contract last November, suspecting you're too old. I probably know every shock you've had. You're not too old, by the way. Let's talk—"

"No, please. All I'm looking for this morning is to find out why you mistrust your wife's conclusion that my Generalized Anxiety Disorder may attract Chronic Fatigue Syndrome, in which case she suspects I'll need to go on disability. She says two milligrams of lorazepam daily can prevent that."

"You'll be hooked on the drug before you know it. But do what you like. She can write your prescription or I can. Gotta go; I'll send Amy in."

He left the door open, lab coat flapping.

Rhonda tried to stand but failed. What she hoped at least to do was crawl to the padded table, drag herself onto it, stretch out, and close her eyes.

Dog

Derek does not want to buy a puppy for his daughter far away, even though his ex believes it can cure her tantrums, but a loose dog he kicks helps to change his mind.

Derek threw his ballpoint at his home-office window. On the other side, a squirrel that had been gobbling the sunflower seeds he'd set out for chickadees leapt up and scrambled out of sight.

The letter he'd been drafting to his ex-wife said neither all he'd wished to nor used the tone he'd been hoping for. Yes, he applauded her plan to buy a puppy for Alicia, their twelve-year-old hellion. Yes, he agreed a dog might do for their daughter what therapy could not. But no way he'd help fund an experiment involving a purebred Cavalier King Charles toy spaniel—we're talking big bucks here—however lauded its reputation for muting the tantrums of children, no matter how much Alicia had fallen in love with the purebred's photo.

The written words sounded cold, a martinet's. His ex knew he feared dogs, knew his uncle's schnauzer had lacerated his ankle when Derek had been just Alicia's age. Plus, he felt uncomfortable around children, his ex knew that, too—so much need to be noticed, so many questions, mopes, illnesses. She'd agreed before they'd married to take precautions. And she'd broken that vow.

He required fresh air to think.

In five minutes he maneuvered his Lexus equally between two of the lines in the nearby park's lot. A breeze rattled leaves of Siberian elms leading to the playground. He hoped nine-thirty was early enough to keep kiddies and their mothers away a while longer, though this morning's lead letter-to-the-editor claimed climate change had made this the warmest November on record.

The sun soothed his neck as he lowered himself to a bench's green slats and stretched his legs. No little bodies yet scrambled up the rope webbing nor wriggled headlong down the slides.

Across the soccer field a van stopped beside the curb. Out hopped a woman in a turban who walked back to free two Afghan hounds. She snapped leashes to their collars and started along the dirt path. Leashes, all right: no problem.

A gust blew a clutch of elm leaves off their twigs. Three settled into his lap as an idea fluttered into his head. Offer to pay Alicia's round-trip from Santa Barbara, take her to view the Santa Fe Shelter's lovable (he supposed) mutts yearning for a home, thus dissuading her from setting her heart on the spaniel.

Pay her fare? Was he also willing to risk sparking a tantrum? Better to offer to finance a mutt and its shots from a shelter in Santa Barbara.

Warmth suffused him. Soon he'd need to drive home, begin the day's four-hour grind of using e-mail and the Web to help clients find higher-paying jobs.

He startled as a yellow bus in front of the community gymnasium disgorged a swarm of children. Like grasshoppers they sprang onto the bark chips and thence the swings, into the polypropylene tunnel, onto the slides, the net, the teeter-totter. Unlike grasshoppers, they squealed, giggled, shouted, and complained. Two girls looked around to make sure their teachers or parents or whatever were following.

He clapped his hands over his ears and started to rise when he felt something nudge his calf. He glanced down. A goddamned, loose dog with a red tag swinging from its collar. What a tangle of hair, even on its paws. Barely a foot high, it sniffed Derek's cuff. *Get away you, don't poop on me.* Derek flung the toe of his loafer into the dog's belly, lifting it off the path. The little guy yelped and scurried behind an elm.

"What'd you do that for, buster?"

"Huh?" Derek looked past his shoulder to see who owned the high voice. A boy in shorts and overhanging shirt stared, hands on hips. His lower lip covered his upper lip and his forehead bore a scar that vanished into a shock of hair.

"You can't treat animals that way."

"Sure I can when they're not leashed. Who you?"

"Nathaniel!" called one of the women. She vacated a bench near the horizontal ladder. "Leave the gentleman alone."

"He kicked a dog."

"That's not your concern. Come back here, please."

"Not until he makes amends."

Amends? The word from a boy seeming about Alicia's age?

"You should find its owner," the youngster said.

"Why don't you do it?"

"Nathaniel."

"You should give it some water."

"Nathaniel, I'll have to go bring Miss Garrison."

"'Change your karma, buster."

"Change my—"

But the boy was hurrying back to the playground.

Meanwhile the animal had started over the footbridge toward the picnic tables and lot.

"Hey, you, hey, dog," Derek called and began to run after it.

The Hug

Ronnie and Sheila have been friends only, but Sheila's husband's affairs and Ronnie's wife's weight may change the friendship—at least so it seems at this particular lunch.

Ronnie had met Sheila on the first of five round-trips from Santa Fe to Lenox, Massachusetts, to earn a low-residency MFA in Fine Arts from Berkshire College. The process took two years.

In Santa Fe Ronnie, a potter, ran a card and gift shop with his wife. Sheila, a monotypist, needn't make money—her husband managed the main branch of First New Mexico Bank.

Ronnie's wife and Sheila's husband didn't know each other well but Ronnie and Sheila lunched every other month at A Little Bit of Sicily to talk art. When either had a show, their spouses exchanged small talk there.

It was a first marriage for each, and each had two kids who'd settled on the coasts. When Sheila shared that her husband had had two affairs she knew about, Ronnie shared that, while tempted, he'd managed to stay faithful, and suspected likewise of his letting-herself-get-a-bit-too-chubby wife, though they'd not made love for months.

Yet Ronnie had rarely fantasized erotically about Sheila. She seemed more an older sister, though he admitted sometimes wishing he could discover if her breasts were as firm as they appeared. Whether she fantasized about him he had not a clue. Their hugs hello and goodbye had felt sexless.

On this particular Monday, across from the bike shop's Styrofoam snowmen and tinsel, end-to-end sisal mats led over ice to the restaurant's entrance. After finishing their minestrone and insalata mista, Sheila—instead of consulting her watch and rising, as she usually did—asked if Ronnie might like another decaf. He discovered himself locking onto her gaze.

The waitress walked over to refill his and Sheila's mugs.

He watched Sheila's heavy, unpenciled brows knit while she sipped, and began posing questions he'd never thought to ask. Was her son happy in his marriage? What courses had Sheila liked most at Northwestern? Why those? What in life did she feel had passed her by?

He suspected they could happily have sat out the afternoon, but supposed his wife would fret that an accident had occurred, that he'd been rear-ended or his car had slid. He flagged the waitress for the check.

Outside, Sheila and he pulled gloves from their coats and stepped gingerly toward the parking lot. At the curb he stopped, turned to her, and, as always, held out his arms.

Today she seemed not to want to let go, and he kissed her cheek. "Icy," he whispered.

She shook black curls threaded with gray. "Until February?" she asked and continued to hold him.

"Maybe sooner?"

"Sooner, Ronnie, yes, I think that might be a whole lot better."

Providence

Rachel guesses right—husband and son berate her for losing her purse at the gym, but she believes far more than they in God's beneficence.

"Who's seen a yellow purse?" Rachel called into the crowd stretching tendons, lifting dumbbells, jumping rope, contracting their abs in the weight room of the gym at Ft. Marcy Complex. "I left it on a bench five minutes ago, I know I did."

Having hurried back from her locked car in the morning's cold, she felt dizzy. A woman chewing gum shook her head; a teenager with orange-spiked hair threw his palms up. The indoor stink of perspiration seemed to have doubled.

In sneakers and sweats, red fleece and knit cap, she next queried the girl under the clock behind the counter.

The girl shrugged massive shoulders.

Where was the blasted thing? Rachel dashed out. It would take at least ten minutes to jog home. Would her son laugh? Mostly she hoped her husband had left for his business breakfast.

Where in the house had she put her emergency keys? Okay, God, she prayed, beginning her run through the parking lot and onto Murales Road, I know You don't like me mentioning specifics but this is a test. Find my keys, please, and find my purse. It's my day to serve lunch to the homeless.

▲▲▲

Her husband's new blue Honda sat in the drive. Rachel stood on the porch until her breathing had slowed, then twisted the doorknob.

Inside was as hot as the gym. Her husband jumped from a chair by the dining table. "Where the hell've you been? My battery's gone dead. Triple A can't come for half an hour and I'm already late. Matthew called Freddie; Freddie's mother will be here any minute. Give me your keys."

Rachel squeezed her eyes shut. "I've lost my purse."

"Huh?"

"God'll find it, Scott."

"Oh, man." He slapped his forehead.

"Mom, jeez, why didn't you lock it in the trunk?"

"Why take it down there at all? Goddamnit son of a bitch."

"Scott, that's not helpful."

"My appointment's in the La Fonda lobby as we speak. He may want me to fly to Austin for two weeks to lead a course on anger management. Largest realtor there. Big bucks, Rachel."

She kept her voice soft. "Do you carry my spare keys on your ring by any chance?"

Scott just stared. "Why do you go to that gym, anyway? They're all purse-snatchers or pickpockets."

"C'mon, Dad, we play basketball there."

"Not in the weight room you don't."

"Of course not in the weight room."

"I haven't a clue what my appointment's cell number is."

"Call the front desk, Scott."

"Don't tell me what to do."

"Dad, that's rude."

"I'll talk to your mother any way...ah."

She let him hug her, raced into their bedroom, opened the dresser's third drawer, and extracted a key chain from under her sweaters.

Scott was on the phone when she hurried back.

A horn sounded and Matthew grabbed his knapsack and the bag lunch Rachel had fixed.

"I'm coming with you," she said.

"To school?"

"To my car."

Rachel waved goodbye but Scott was scowling at an iPhone.

▲▲▲

Freddie's mother stopped next to Rachel's secondhand Prius and Rachel stepped out.

"Mom, why do you take your purse into the gym?" Matthew called from the backseat.

"My mother carried a yellow purse. She never let it leave her sight. Thanks a bunch, Margaret."

Rachel crossed the lot, walked over the wooden bridge, passed the playground equipment, and waited for the gym doors to slide back.

"Has a purse turned up yet?" she asked the girl beneath the clock.

"Color?"

"Yellow."

"Dude just dropped it off." Shoulders lowered, the girl reached under the counter.

The back of Rachel's neck prickled as she rummaged through it. Money all there. Credit cards. Address book, cell phone, keys.

She held the purse to her chest and patted it. *You see, Scott?*

Nice Try

Just before delivering a Valentine's Day gift to his hoped-for girlfriend, Hugh falls from his bicycle, but the girl's mother says she would like the muddy mess herself, as the husband watches.

Yes, Hugh had a license but no, he didn't want the Miata convertible his father had offered the down payment on for a seventeenth-birthday gift.

As founder and president of Green Teens, he preferred to bicycle, not one of those sixteen-gear, carbon, fiber jobs but the three-gear, used Schwinn he peddled now.

It was Valentine's Day and Hugh was wheezing up Camino De Cruz Blanca towards Daphne's folks' probable mansion—tucked away, she'd told him, off Garcia Lane—to deliver the red sack he'd packed with ginger, candied prickly pear, and two jars of mesquite-bean jelly, tied off with a golden bow.

He hoped the gift would loosen her stated commitment to the soccer team's captain enough to say yes on joining him next Saturday for lunch at the Cowgirl BBQ, even though that meant needing to borrow one of his parents' cars.

What a gorgeous morning, the air pungent with ponderosas. But all this pumping seemed to be swelling his bladder. Did he want to ask the Mackervilles if he might use their bathroom? No thanks. He hoped to set the sack—riding in a shoebox tied to his Schwinn—on their doormat if there was one, ring the bell, and get the hell out.

What to do? A pickup carrying windows strapped to an aluminum A-frame rattled downhill. He spied the sign for Garcia Lane just upside a home fronted by woolly-stemmed chamisa. Perhaps he could relieve himself unseen between a couple of the bushes.

He braked, stopped, dismounted, and stepped over a chunk of snow.

He could only think to grin as a white Mercedes SUV sped uphill and the woman wearing a Stetson on the passenger side waved.

Minutes later he turned onto a muddy, down-sloping drive that disappeared to the left.

Uh-oh: that white Mercedes he'd just seen sat in front of three garage doors faced with random-length planks. Wrapped in a multihued Joseph's coat, the woman was stepping out. Small, pert nose—like Daphne's. A man with the shoulders of a wrestler slammed the driver's door shut.

"Well, hello," called the woman.

Hugh skidded to miss a pothole and fell.

She ran over, pressing her Stetson down with one hand, while he stood his bike on its stand and began brushing slush from his hip.

"Are you all right?"

Hugh nodded.

"You are who?" She smelled deliciously of jasmine.

"Hugh Dillard, ma'am, a friend of Daphne's."

The big man lumbered close.

"We're just home from church," she said. "Mind my asking what you were doing back there?"

"Well, yeah—no. We've a botany project to find out which plants are waterwise. I'm in charge of chamisa."

The man, dressed in cashmere jacket, crewneck, and tooled boots, gray hair sheared to a quarter-inch of his scalp, thrust out a paw. "John Mackerville."

"Hi there, Mr. Mackerville."

The woman raised the hem of her coat to mid-calf. "I'll go see if Daphne's home."

"No, please. She didn't know I was coming. I brought her—oh, brother—this."

The wet sack had leapt from its shoebox to fall under the back wheel's sprocket. Mushed prickly pear darkened the red sack. He felt its sides and drew his fingertips off hidden shards of glass. "Happy Valentine's Day. The mesquite-bean jelly's smashed."

"Mesquite bean? How thoughtful! She'll be thrilled."

"I doubt it."

"Of course she will. More than if nothing had broken."

"Like my heart?"

"Why, you darling boy. Come in—you must."

Hugh tossed shoulder-length hair, crowned by a knit cap. "No way, ma'am."

"But..."

Hugh bent to lift the sack free. "You want this mess?"

"In place of what my husband forgot about? Sure I do."

Gotcha

When Rod plays a trick on Jimbo for embarrassing him in public before they broke up, the woman Rod tells Jimbo he's going to marry decides to take him seriously.

Jimbo worked at Merrill Lynch, Rod at Smith Barney, and for two years they'd been housemates and lovers. But Rod began to binge on junk food and when he got so fat that Jimbo in public started calling him Jumbo, Rod moved out to go live with the grandmother who'd raised him.

Her hugs and vegetables from her garden coaxed him off the tortilla chips and back into shape.

A month ago Virginia, a receptionist at Merrill Lynch, applied for and got the same job for more money at Smith Barney. There she found herself falling for the slimmed-down Rod, though her therapist reminded her that *triangle* equals *time bomb*, particularly when it includes parted lovers.

A week ago Jimbo had seen Rod on one of the benches at the Plaza, eating from the lunchbox his grandmother sent out with him mornings. Jimbo had winced, recalling the warmth of their nights together, the Sunday walks among cottonwoods along Big Tesuque Creek. When he returned to the office, he'd phoned Rod.

▲▲▲

Jimbo and Rod now sat in the courtyard of the Rio Chama Restaurant. Ivy-strewn walls and a canopy overhead shielded them and other diners from street noise and the sun's heat. Both men had ordered the Daily Grind burger with sweet potato fries. Rod sipped a Pellegrino.

"You're a good boy to agree to this," Jimbo enthused. "I've missed you, chum."

"It's been hard for me, too, Jimbo."

"You're looking to die for. Any possibility, you think?"

"Of?"

"Say trying a Sunday hike together?"

"I'll have to think about that. Here come our lunches and I need to use the *Men's*. Back in a sec."

Rod glanced at his chromium time/date/sunrise-and-moonrise wristwatch. She should have arrived.

And she had. Virginia stood outside *Ladies*, slinky in the orange sheath she'd come to work in. Rod felt his penis stirring. Huh? For a woman? This was new. "Ready?" he asked.

She followed him past a display of Native American pots to the table.

"Virginia!" Jimbo blurted.

Rod dipped his face to sniff his fries. "We wanted to surprise you, Jim. Virginia and I are planning to marry."

"Marry?" Jimbo's heavy brows leapt.

"After lunch we're heading to Santa Fe Goldworks to look for a ring."

"Ring?"

"Engagement ring, you know what that is. Virginia says she'd like to join us for lunch first."

"She does?"

"Super. What would you like to eat, sweetheart?"

Rod sat, bit into his burger, and put his arm around Jimbo's shoulder. "Just kidding about the marriage, pal. What a sport this gal is."

But why was her warm palm settling on his thigh?

Parenting

Instead of physically attacking Amanda's father, Amanda's mother takes a butcher knife to the teddy bear he bought.

"Don't fight, don't fight," Amanda called out, clutching the teddy bear her father had brought home yesterday.

"We're not fighting, punkin."

"Of course we are," her mother said, two inches taller than Amanda's father and, unlike him, still with a full head of hair.

Mother and father faced each other across a mahogany island laden with a butcher knife, green bowl of oranges, and a slab of filet mignon.

Amanda waited in a corner of the kitchen, dressed in a pinafore for kindergarten—chin lowered but eyes vigilant, pressing the backs of her arms against the furnace-warmed plaster. The room smelled more of the morning's maple syrup than tonight's steak.

"Gotta get moving," her father said. "Throw Smoky on the bed and grab your sweater, princess."

"Are you going to pick up the capers or not?" her mother asked.

"Not. You forgot them. You've got the morning, I've got Amanda to drop off and an eight forty-five at Thornberg Investment—we're talking a sale of maybe sixteen scanners."

"I don't have the morning, my sister's flying in."

"Not my problem."

"Your problem if you put your hands all over her again. How about on your way home?"

"How about on *your* way home?"

"Stop it, stop it," Amanda cried out but stayed put in her warm corner.

Her father picked up his briefcase and laptop. "Get your goddamned sweater, Amanda, c'mon."

"How dare you talk to her that way?"

"This is stupid," he said.

"You aren't kidding. How about this? Yvonne will be here until after her show on Friday. I'll pick up the capers if you'll do the cooking."

"I always cook when your sister comes."

"Smoky," Amanda said to her teddy, "tell them to make up."

"Make up what?" her father asked.

"Quit harassing her," Amanda's mother said.

"Harassing whom, sweetheart?" her father said to her mother.

Amanda's mother pivoted, grabbed the knife off the island, snatched the bear from Amanda, slit open its belly, threw the knife to the counter, and began to haul out the bear's stuffing. "It's time to impress on your father that he needs to change his behavior."

Hypertrichosis Meets Clérambault's Syndrome

Star, a young beauty, has fallen for the professor who teaches Dante's Inferno, but wonders why he wears long sleeves in such hot weather.

"What's this?"

Professor Jason Mulgraves had released the students from his seminar on the *Paradiso*. But one student, Star Janz, had hung back to hand him an envelope.

"Me to you, Mr. Mulgraves." The young beauty's scent of honeysuckle and alcohol made him dizzy. Her ironed hair hung halfway to her waist, her nipples must surely rise upward—arms she left uncovered (unlike his own), nose narrow and straight as that of the faux-marble Aphrodite on the table behind him....

Her green eyes held his until he looked away.

"I want you to open it as soon as you can."

"Now?"

"Alone."

Her voice filled him with the hum of insects in his garden.

"Can you give me a hint of its contents?"

She looked down at the sheer cotton hiding the belt loops of her denims, and tucked a golden sheaf of hair behind her ear. "I'd rather you read it."

"At lunch soon enough?"

She nodded. "Aren't you hot in that shirt?"

"A bit."

"You're frowning."

"Oh?" He attempted to clear his forehead. "I've worn long sleeves since high school. Habit, I guess."

"I'd like to talk about the letter later."

"Of course." Had his frown betrayed his yearning? Other co-eds had thanked him for his enthusiasm for Dante, even asked if they might talk somewhere off-campus. Always he'd declined.

"My office at three?"

"Thank you, sir." Star grabbed her text, notebook, and laptop from the table and hurried out.

Sir? Rarely did he hear the word used, though he'd been teaching for a quarter century.

He captured the envelope between both palms and held it as in prayer to his nose. A bit of scent lingered.

That he drank himself into blackouts most nights no one knew except his doctor. Likewise that the backs of his arms, calves and under his thighs, his back, belly, and chest to his collarbone, were matted, like a wolf's, with hair. His doctor called the condition hypertrichosis, and suggested that if he cut back on his drinking, the hair—triggered probably by porphyrins in the liver—might drop away.

Cut back? Ho, ho, ha. The ritual of following a series of old-fashioneds with sipping whiskey poured from the bed table gave him reason for living. Icy showers and three Tylenols before bicycling to work kept him functioning just fine, thank you.

▲▲▲

Star's letter lay open in front of the vegan burrito and Styrofoam cup of tea he'd brought in from the cafeteria.

"My darling," it began.

"Your smile is my sun. How you gaze at me when I share in class is like you've locked me in your arms. Last month during our student conference, I watched you lean forward and couldn't help aching below. Hopefully you noticed nothing. I want to get to know you, hear about your childhood, learn why you've never married (I've been snooping around, you see), show how I can make you happy, Jason. We are..."

Clérambault's syndrome, no question—he'd Googled *erotomania* a year ago when a student had grasped his hand. But he realized, reading Star's letter, he'd started panting, that his zipper had stretched taut, and he threw down his fist, arcing a spray of tea onto the desk blotter.

The hair on his arms and chest begin to itch. He glanced at his father's pocket watch hanging in the bell jar on a bookcase opposite and rehearsed what, in half an hour, he'd say aloud.

No, Star, this is a delusion. I have no attraction for you. Please ask Counseling to direct you to a psychiatrist or I shall have to ask the president's office to contact your parents. At least I shall find myself forced to request your transfer from the seminar.

But what if she didn't care that he was furred? That so much hair turned her on even more?

Foul

Isabel, having just had her first period, doesn't yet know her divorced father's secret, but does intend to teach him to stop treating her like a boy.

Twelve-year-old Isabel's dad, Tom Atkinson, had been a star guard for the Milwaukee Bucks before pulling up stakes for Santa Fe.

After last spring's divorce here, Isabel and her younger brother, Sammy, stayed with Tom every other weekend. He'd purchased a southside adobe because its previous owner, to seat a Lincoln Navigator and tow-along camper, had laid a slab the length of the house.

Two weeks ago, Tom had rented a couple of posthole diggers, and bought a bag of cement and two poles, hoops, and nets. The kids and he—with help from the neighbor across the street—created holes three feet deep, bolted hoops to the poles, secured their free ends in cement, and braced them with two-by-fours.

Yesterday Isabel and Sammy had mostly practiced dribbling. Tom had never seen his daughter so clumsy, though his ex had warned him that Isabel no longer wanted to be thought a tomboy. Wednesday she'd had her first period.

This Sunday morning, in the warm breeze, Tom's neighbor was hosing down his pickup when Tom, Sammy, and Isabel emerged onto the front porch. Tom—who now made a living selling solar panels—carried the ball, wearing the jersey of his days as a pro. Ten-year-old Sammy wore black shorts that covered his knees. Isabel followed in a training bra whose spandex peeped out across the neckline of a sleeveless sundress. Tom and his son wore sneakers, Isabel flats.

"Hustle, gang," Tom said, waving to his neighbor, then dribbling down the steps and crossing the yard onto the slab. The new hoops and poles shimmered in the fall light.

Tom tousled Isabel's hair, part of which fell over her chest and part over her back.

"Dad, please."

"It's going to muss up when you play, butch."

"You know I hate your calling me that."

"I think it's funny. You want to practice dribbling before we start?"

Isabel swore to teach her father a lesson. "Let's get going. I promised to text my best friend, Elizabeth, at eleven."

"Ball up," their father said, holding it level with his crew cut. "Ready?"

He thrust it into the air and backed off. Sammy grabbed it, feinted to his right, and when Isabel lurched to steal it away, Sammy shifted left, dribbled toward the street, and leapt. The ball bounced off the hoop's rim.

Isabel snatched it on its second bounce and began to race toward the back fence.

"No!" her father shouted. "You have to dribble. Free throw for Sam." Tom stepped forward but she ducked to throw her shoulder against the side of his knee and he went down.

She neared the rear hoop and, dress flapping, tossed the ball up from her waist with both hands. It swished through the net.

When she turned, Sammy and the neighbor—a burly man with tight curls and the tattoo of a buffalo on his forearm—had crouched beside her father. She could hear her father's groans. Serves him right, she thought, but as she walked toward them, she started to cry.

The neighbor lifted her father's head.

Wait a minute, that was her or Sammy's job!

What she and Sammy didn't yet know was that her father and the neighbor had become quite fond of each other—had, in fact, become lovers.

Second Choice

After long absence, at his high school reunion Luke finds himself next to the woman who had threatened to kill herself if he wouldn't marry her—as well as beside the other old-woman-now he'd been so crazy about.

At his high school reunion, Luke Waters, a lifelong bachelor, again found himself holding the hand of Tatiana who, long ago at the prom, had sworn to take her life by swallowing a handful of her mother's meds if Luke didn't propose marriage that evening.

He'd pleaded a latent love for boys, when in truth the homecoming queen, Julie Finlay, herself engaged to the school's tennis captain, dominated his fantasies.

The next morning Tatiana had done as she'd vowed—then freaked, found the castor oil her mother used as an emetic, and stayed alive. Two days later Luke's father had moved his own family overseas, where he began managing the Bristol office of Lloyds of London.

So how did Tatiana come to be pressing herself against seventy-two-year-old Luke Waters? In a wiggy moment he'd phoned her, following a search on the Internet. They'd not talked since the late fifties. Married once, no children, she'd driven up from Albuquerque. He discovered he liked her better now, stunning in a black dress and black jacket embroidered with wisteria. Her whine had vanished. She wore none of the heavy perfume he remembered. Nor had she—unlike most of the women milling about—a triple chin.

The six members of the band, classmates all, settled in their chairs for some pre-dinner music-making. Couples sauntered to the middle of the floor in the La Fonda's top-story ballroom.

"Like to?" he asked Tatiana.

"Love to, Luke, but..." She set fingertips on his collar. "Decades of trauma have given me a nervous tummy. After you phoned, my doctor suggested easy does it."

"Shall we choose a table, then?"

"Whatever you like. I'm just happy this all is happening."

Luke spotted a woman sitting alone. Three strands of pearls graced her neck, pearls her ears, and a silvered perm her high forehead. "May we?" he asked.

"Of course."

That contralto. Could it be...? He pulled the folding chair out for Tatiana and saw the woman glance at the plasticized name card dangling over his shirt. "Luke Waters? Hello." She peered past him. "Hello, Tatiana."

"Julie Finlay?"

"You got her."

Luke's neck prickled. Chestnut-colored, half-moon brows—he should have guessed. She didn't look a bit like the girl of his fantasies. Simply a meticulously groomed old lady.

Tatiana gripped the elbow of Luke's blazer and bent forward. "You're as gorgeous as ever, Julie. How do you do it?"

"Hours of prep."

"How long ago did you lose Howard?" Tatiana asked.

"We broke up the summer of graduation. He died in a hit-and-run months later, after starting at New Mexico State. Howie never loved me. He had a crush on *you*. I suppose you never knew; I sure didn't. After you took those pills, he kept calling out *Tatiana* in his sleep. So you two got back together after Luke returned from London? But why no wedding rings?"

Far Away

Husband Brad can't understand why Ursula, suffering from rheumatoid arthritis and long bored by the physics he teaches, spends so much time watching astronauts maneuver above the earth on NASA's channel 212.

Early in January, Brad took the morning off from teaching physics at Santa Fe High to hear the doctor say how his wife Ursula might best cope with the pains in her elbows from the first stage of rheumatoid arthritis.

On a Sunday two weeks later, Ursula cocooned herself in one of the living-room's lounge chairs and covered her lap with the golden throw her mother had knit long ago. A matching knit cap hid her still-thick, chestnut-colored hair, knotted, as usual, into a bun.

She muted the remote and in the dusk stared at NASA's Channel 212. Commander Jeff Williams, wearing padded white gear resembling a diver's, was floating two hundred and twenty miles above earth through the International Space Station's "Harmony" module.

Ursula hadn't heard Brad tramping down the stairway. She startled as his palm settled on her shoulder.

"No sound?" he asked.

"Isn't it lovely? Look, here comes Specialist Stephen Robinson."

A second astronaut floated into view from the module housing life-support equipment. He grabbed hold of a rack overflowing with blue-and-white cable and propelled himself toward Commander Jeff. The two men gripped hands and raised them in a howdy to viewers.

"I'm sure," said Ursula, "our military hopes to use what these guys learn, and I know the billions this project costs could better be spent in defusing the population bomb, stamping out TB in Africa, whatever—and you know what? I don't care.

"I love watching these jokers drift around modules with their never-never-land names—Harmony, Sunrise, Unity, Destiny, Hope, and pretty soon Tranquility with its seven-window observation deck—describing what they're doing to benefit mankind. They talk to groups of kindergarteners, too, showing off their uniforms, sharing how they keep breakfast eggs from rising off the plates, explaining—"

"Jesus, Ursula!" Brad swiped the side of his head. "When did you get so interested in science? I've worked my ass off for twelve years teaching high-school physics and bet in all that time you haven't asked three questions, not even, 'How did your day go?'"

"Brad—"

"Shut up a minute. So maybe I'm not that keen on hearing everything you're asked at the reference desk. But when you said you're being considered for head librarian at the downtown branch, I gave you a hug, didn't I?"

"Yes, you did."

"So?"

"It felt good, Brad."

"That's all?"

She clutched her left elbow as pain shot through it. "What else should I have done?"

The Black Cat

Andrew's buddy said that Honor would sleep with any guy, so long as he smelled okay, but she wants to drink at a gay bar first.

Andrew's buddy Alexey had told him about Honor, and Andrew had called her up, invited her to dinner.

Condoms wrapped in his handkerchief, he stabbed the buzzer to her casita, tucked behind the main house on Cerro Gordo. Honeysuckle lazed along wires flanking the path and a plum in full bloom overhung the roof, sweetening the air.

The door opened to a woman in her twenties, prettier than Andrew had imagined and looking far less used. Blonde ringlets bounced off her shoulders. Her light-blue eyes held his as she asked him in. She wore a white blouse ruffled toward the collar, dreamcatcher earrings woven of silver, and slacks that matched her eyes. Flat tummy, thin wrists.

Andrew couldn't believe his good fortune. All this for a dinner out? Acid burnt his throat as he remembered the break-up breakfast with Claire—her claim that two years of sex with him had convinced her to try a few overnights with women. He'd bought an engagement ring just two days prior.

"Sit, please," Honor said. A pressed-coffee-grounds Java Log flamed in the corner fireplace. A couple of nearly-abstract landscapes—orange dribbles and adobe-brown slashes—hung above the rattan armchair Andrew chose.

"Do you paint?" he asked, pointing up.

"Ex-boyfriend." She curled her feet under her thigh on a loveseat upholstered in orange leather.

"Hungry?" he asked.

"Not yet."

No drinks, no snacks? She wanted to go at it now? His mind rearranged words to speak, phrases. Alexey had explained that Honor had never been able to climax with a man inside her, including himself. She was searching for a soulmate, proof being the guy who freed her to come. She'd sleep with anyone, Alexey said, so long as he dressed sharply and smelled okay.

Andrew had taken the flared-collar shirt he wore now to Martinizing for a wash and press, likewise his khakis. He hoped she liked the Gucchi Pour Homme he'd splashed on.

"You're biting your lip," she said and twisted a ringlet behind an ear.

Might as well be as direct. "Want to get to know each other in your bedroom?"

"Let's start at The Black Cat."

"What's that?"

"Never heard of The Black Cat?"

"Never." Though did he recall Alexey saying something in passing?

"Hangout on Second Street past Chocolate Maven, near where Cloud Cliff Bakery was. Green Zone for the out-of-the-closet crowd."

"You're gay?"

"I feel safe there. No hombres coming on to me. What's your name again?"

"I'm Andrew Timmerman."

"Well, Andrew," she said, rising and extending her hands, "Let's go see what the night has in store for us, shall we?"

Reality Check

When Miles at age 41 leaves his barren wife for someone who can give him children, the candidate he chooses harbors a discouraging secret.

Though somewhat concerned that the world's population was racing toward nine billion, Miles felt that siring children and *their* siring children could comfort him with the myth of immortality.

Which is why last year, at age forty-one, he left his barren, chain-smoking wife and went on the prowl.

"May I bring you a refill?" he asked the woman he'd grabbed the chair next to at the April homeowners' meeting. He and she owned adjacent townhouses up the hill. When he returned from his daily grind as a tax attorney, often he'd see her walking her whippet along the side of the road, in which case he'd slow and wave.

She twisted in her folding chair to look at him, and he marveled up close at the satiny and fragrant fall of brown hair that shimmied about her shoulders. No wrinkles, no ring other than the topaz on her right hand. She firmed her lips, tilted her head to the side, and said, "Sure."

"Sweetener? Creamer?"

"Black."

He took their cups as the association's president, decked in red tartan and a Ralph Lauren polo, began a harangue on the need to raise dues. "Because our UPS and Fed Ex friends are tearing up the roads in spite of the speed humps your board authorized last fall. Because scale on the piñons needs to be sprayed. Because..."

"I'm Miles Davis," Miles whispered, returning with their coffees.

"Are you joking?"

He loved that laugh—throaty, full of delight. She'd make a fine mother. Had she kids already, he wondered? He leaned closer, sorry she'd pinched shut her blouse's top. "The musician's is my name, too."

God, the way her hair smelled, like what? The field of mustard he and childhood chums used to swing above from the branch of a eucalyptus.

"Shall we raise our hands?" he asked her when the president called for a vote.

"Let's."

"The ayes have it," the president said. "Thank you, everyone."

Most of the group stood. Some headed for biscuits and cheese, others knotted to talk. "I'm wondering if I might buy you lunch sometime," Miles said.

"Why not?"

"What's your name?"

"Holly Miles."

"With an i?"

"My maiden name, I'm using it again."

"But that's amazing: Miles and Miles."

"Sorry, I have to rush. She shook his hand, turned, and strode toward the double doors.

Feeling downright lightheaded, he angled through the crowd to where the president, road-and-grounds-maintenance volunteer, secretary, and treasurer sat at a long table.

That evening as he flossed, he noticed a light in Holly's bathroom window. He fetched a folding stool, placed it in the bathtub, flicked out the light, and climbed up just in time to see through the transom her lifting off a wig.

His Peacock

Since Yolanda's husband Luis has died, her rich Anglo neighbor keeps asking her out, as persistent as the peacock who invades the privacy of her barbed-wired back yard.

Though still trim, braiding her hair to her waist, proud of the mole to the right of her lips (Luis had called it her beauty spot), Yolanda kept refusing invitations from her Anglo neighbor to share conversation at the Haagen-Dazs ice cream parlor on the Plaza.

Gone now three years after his motorcycle skidded into a phone pole, Luis had sold junk from under the New Mexican locusts in their backyard.

To loops of old hose and piles of warped plywood, Yolanda kept adding hubcaps she pried from cars parked near the Anglo haciendas she cleaned for a living. The stolen caps sparkled among Luis's lengths of pipe and rusting railroad track, tractor tires, a camper top, rolls of fencing, concrete blocks, half a dozen chains hanging low on the shed.

Monuments for his memorial park now, not items to sell or trade—certainly not to provide perches and crappers for the Anglo neighbor's recently-purchased peacock.

The barbed wire she'd paid the son of one of her customers to string between her lot and the Anglo's was useless. The bird had discovered an opening through a wild-branched hedge of creosote bush that backed the neighbor's lot and Yolanda's.

The Anglo, who had just reroofed his home and two-car garage with tile, who owned an auto-parts store here and another in Albuquerque, had always spoken with courtesy to Luis. But Luis he was not, was, in fact, Anglo, and was mistreating Yolanda's privacy.

So this spring morning, when—clutching bucket, window spray, cleanser, and mop—she left the porch's slab for the lean-to that shaded her pickup, and saw the bird's topknots bobbing between the creosote's black branches, she decided *enough*. She set down her fluids, bucket, and mop, stepped through the tangle of pigweed and hairy-leaf kochia, hefted a few stones and railway spikes into her bucket, and retreated onto the slab.

The peacock trailed a magnificence. Its neck feathers also shimmered, its beak jerked forward with each arrogant step, occasionally dipping to pluck a grasshopper from the weeds.

Though she feared pushing her cleaning jobs into late afternoon, thus delaying dinner, and so courting insomnia after snatching half an hour of TV, Yolanda stayed put.

The bird marched between a cracked loop of hose and length of train track. At ten feet away, it shook its pom-poms and cocked its head so that a single, round, midnight-blue eye fixed her.

The spike she hurled was low; the rusted steel knocked one of the bird's thighs.

It shuddered and marched closer.

Gripping a stone, she raised her arm and flung it forward. But the missile dropped short as the peacock let out a mating scream and raised its rear quills to hoist its plumage. Dozens of feather eyes—blue, green, orange, yellow—stared her down.

She overturned her bucket, grabbed the mop, cleanser, and window spray, and hurried toward her truck.

The peacock locked its fan on her like radar as she gunned the engine and spun back over the drive. The proud peafowl strutted right into the flying gravel, screeching Yolanda off her own land.

Muddled

Their daughter has so rattled Arnold and Rosie—news that her husband is gambling away their granddaughters' college-education fund—that the old folks nearly miss their plane.

Arnold and Rosie, Santa Feans in their late seventies, wondered if they'd ever visit the northwest again.

To say goodbye, their daughter and granddaughters had stood on the porch under the wisteria of a two-story clapboard outside McMinnville, Oregon. The seven-year-old held the cat. The open garage showed a jumble of cartons, rakes, Rob's rowing machine, stacks of books for the upcoming community-college fund-raiser. No room for a car; Rob had bicycled earlier than usual to work. His Prius and the family van waited on the drive beside the Mustang the oldsters had rented.

Two-hour naps plus antianxiety meds had helped justify the trip's expense. Arnold and Rosie had enjoyed playing board games with the girls, visiting their schools, watching them dive into the hotel pool. But during the five days, only yesterday had they found the chance to talk with their daughter alone. She claimed Rob was gambling away on professional hockey the girls' college-education fund. He had also begun staying overnight in Portland, last week twice. Divorce seemed likely.

The visitors happily reached the Portland airport in less than an hour. Distraught by his wife's alternating need to curse Rob and wring her hands, Arnold drove down into *Short Term Parking*. Doubling back to *Rentals* took another quarter hour. They hurried out and crossed the throughway into the terminal, slowing when Rosie's left knee started giving way.

They moved through the airline's check-in line until reaching the counter. Arnold lifted his wheeled bag.

"No, sir, it goes over there. Our conveyor belt has rolled over dead." The agent pointed to a mountain of luggage across the hall. "You've got your boarding pass?"

"Yes, yes," Rosie answered for her husband.

Arnold's face grew hot. "Do I sign anything? We're awful late."

"Touch the screen."

"The what?"

"Let me have your pass."

"Where'd you put it, Arnold?"

"Hold on." He rummaged each pocket, remembered he'd tucked it into his shirt, unbuttoned the top, and drew the pass out.

The agent leaned forward, inserted it below the monitor, pressed the screen in a couple of places, handed the pass back. "Yours, ma'am?"

She handed it over.

"Now walk over to *CX Three*, there where the sign reads *Entrance*. Next?"

A harried Native American displaying the airline's badge asked, "Are those bags locked?" Both arms bore eagle tattoos.

The noise from pedestrians and carts zipping past seemed deafening. Rosie stood on tiptoes to bring her lips to Arnold's ear. "Are the *bags locked*?" He'd promised her to purchase hearing aids before year's end.

"Zipped," he said.

"That's good enough." The attendant tossed the bags onto the heap.

"Now what do we do?" Arnold asked.

The mountainous attendant stared a moment. "You go through Security and find your plane. A couple of hints. The planes now are larger than you may remember and they're usually parked outdoors."

Emergency

Elinor finally dares to tell her husband that she's through with cooking—but also, wincing, that the pain in her side she's kept secret for six months is getting worse.

*E*linor set down a platter holding a chunk of iceberg lettuce and beans speckled with bell pepper.

"What's this?" Eddie asked his wife.

"Tonight's blue plate special."

The soon-to-go May sun stretched its beams along the table. Eddie pinched up a bean and nibbled. "Hardly warm."

"We're simplifying." Elinor brought her own platter from the counter and, wincing, sat catercorner to him.

He peeled off a shred of lettuce, dropped it. "I can't eat this."

"Then don't." She spread her paper napkin and scooped up a forkful of beans.

"No A-One? No dressing?"

"I told you when the kids left home I was through cooking."

"Three years ago, Elinor!"

"When you retired from wholesaling refrigerators and we let the gardener go, you took over the yard. I felt guilty quitting cooking then." She began to chew.

"But this is unacceptable." He shoved his platter to the center of the table. Beans sloshed across the porcelain toward her vase of zinnias. He pushed back his chair, stood, and fingered some stubble. "I'm hungry."

"And I'm easing out as chef, Eddie."

"But I hate to cook."

"How would you know?"

"I hated even heating soup before we married."

"In a week you'll be happily fixing every meal. Remember I like my eggs runny. How about this? I'll keep doing the dishes."

"I've got to sit," Eddie managed.

"Please do."

"Your voice sounds tight. Are you all right?" he asked.

"I woke from my nap with a pain in my right side.

"What kind of pain?"

"Like appendicitis."

"That's been taken care of."

"You think I've forgotten?"

"Your side still hurts?"

"Pretty bad."

"But how can you seem so calm? I'm gonna drive you to the ER."

"No."

"No? Why?" He left his chair and gripped her shoulders from behind.

"It's been hurting on and off for six months. Maybe my journey with you is nearly over."

"That's crazy talk, Elinor."

"Crazy or not, no hospital. I'd rather endure at home."

"Horseshit." He dashed to the wall phone and dialed 911. "Why didn't you tell me six months ago? Good God."

"You know you never like to hear me complain."

"Not true."

"Of course it is," she said, bending as the pain sharpened.

"Emergency!" he shouted into the receiver.

It's Official

Charlene's kids aren't sure they're glad she's home, once again, from Soothing Waters Hospital, even when she shows them a certificate officially signed.

"Snowing, always snow when I get home." Charlene threw her peacoat over the arm of the sofa, ripped off her stocking cap, and brushed her fingertips—nails bitten to the quick—back through red hair cut too short, too goddamn short, every time, every time.

"You know that's a falsehood, Charlie," said twin sister Anne, who'd picked her up with the red suitcase that now sat between Charlene's knees.

Charlene scowled. "No falsehood, no way." She brushed the slush from around the suitcase's handle.

"Yesterday was sunny, Mommy."

"So was the day before."

Charlene gazed at her children, Benji and Mary Beth. They stood in the far corner beside the grandfather clock that Charlene had insisted on keeping after her husband, Ben, had told her he'd put up with her nagging long enough. He'd brought the clock home a month earlier, saying it never talked back.

Charlene wondered if Ben had gone on to marry someone else. "No hug hello for Mommy?" she asked.

Mary Beth locked her fingers in front of her dress; Benji kept two of his between his lips.

"They're shy," her sister said.

"Shy? To hug their mother? That's wrong, it's all wrong."

"You've been gone two weeks."

"Get out of my way." Charlene stepped past the suitcase.

"Take it easy with them, Charlie."

"Who are you, Miss Spinster Winster with her show-off new Pontiac, to tell me what to do?" Charlene faced her look-alike except for the birthmark that discolored Anne's jaw like a squashed raspberry.

"I'm just trying to help."

"I know that, darling, I know that!" Charlene pulled her sister close. Melted snow on the back of Anne's long coat wet her palms. Charlene's battered Chevy sat on a slab under the tarp Anne had bought the first time Charlene had signed herself into Soothing Waters Hospital, following Ben's about-face.

Charlene gave Anne a final squeeze and ran to the children. "Mommy's home, Mommy's home." She lifted Benji and laid her cold cheek against his hot one. "Are you glad?"

"Um hmm," he said.

She set him down and knelt on the braided throw. "What about you, sugarplum?"

"I think so," Mary Beth said.

"Think so? Know so. C'mon." She brought Mary Beth's lips to hers.

The eight-year-old drew away and wiped off the kiss. "How long are you staying?"

"Forever and ever!"

"You're well, then?" Mary Beth asked.

Charlene held up a forefinger, stood, hurried to her suitcase, and unsnapped its latches. "Take a gander, kids. It's official."

She laid the halves of the suitcase flat, dug under a couple of sweaters, and produced a sheet of cardboard. "All the way better, you see? That's the assistant director's signature in the corner but I wrote the certificate out and colored the border."

SAIN, the inch-high capitals read.

Sorting Out Monday Morning

Memory, that ringmaster, spins the aging minds of Winnie and Jonathan like tops.

"Didn't we have a merry old time yesterday?" Winnie asked her husband, Jonathan. Having descended in her robe, she joined him for the last of his breakfast. "Seeing the two magpie nests in the cottonwoods and hearing all those red wings singing."

"The blackbirds."

"The blackbirds, yes, Jonathan."

"You're up earlier than usual, aren't you?"

"Rejunvenated, sugarbun."

"Good to know." He tipped his bowl to shovel up a last spoonful of Grape-Nuts and a raspberry. "Got to brush and be on my walk before the sun starts in."

"Jonathan?"

"What?" He was heading for the stairs.

"Do you recall what time Javier is due?"

"I didn't know he was coming."

"To replace the cupboards' broken hinges. You called him."

"I did?"

"Saturday. Friday? Maybe yesterday, before our picnic."

"Oh, sure. Not the hinges, though. First we tackle the outdoor stuff."

"You're both working on outdoor projects? What about your heart?"

"Not *we* literally. He needs to drive to Classic Rock—let's see. Southwest Landscape. Pick up gravel and spread it on the drive. Then he needs to…wash the windows, I believe."

"Did you write it down? May I see the list, please?

"Didn't I give you a copy?"

"I don't believe so."

"I always do."

"Not this time."

"It's probably on my desk."

"You go brush your teeth. Where on your desk?"

"One of the piles. Left side if he's coming this morning. Right side if it's a different morning."

"It's today, sugarbun. Eight o'clock, I think you said."

"Maybe the other way round, right-hand pile if today, left-hand for a different day."

"I'll find it." Winnie started to pass him but he gripped her elbow.

"I may have put it in a yellow folder, top drawer. Reminder to start on repairs before the real heat hits."

"Weather doesn't matter for inside chores like hinges, does it?"

"No, but I suspect I listed half a dozen jobs for outside first."

"Yellow folder, then."

"Probably."

"Top drawer. Left or right?"

"Right—no, wait. The side my heart's on." He clapped his right breast, switched hands. "Left drawer. Look at the time!"

"Where are you heading so early? The bank doesn't open until nine. Of course, the gravel shop."

"It's not a shop."

"Whatever it is."

"Anyway, I'm not going, Javier's going. He's the one with the pickup. If today's the day."

"For what, sugarbun?" Winnie paused in the doorway to his office.

"For outdoor repairs."

"Dumb me. You'll show him what to do and then be off."

"Off?"

"To the bank or wherever you're going. Now why am I standing here?"

"You—"

"To find the checkbook? You can find it, surely."

"I may have removed it from the cubby in order to—"

"Take it with you when you leave?"

"What reason would I have for that?"

"I don't know, I'm sure."

"But I know why, I mean would know, if I needed to leave. Could have put the checkbook in the yellow folder, not to forget."

"To pay Javier?"

"That's it! May have, may not. Have I taken my walk? Couldn't have."

"Oh?"

"I'm still in slippers."

"I recall your also saying something about your teeth. Do you need to schedule a cleaning? But would the office be open yet, Jonathan?"

"By eight-thirty? Sure thing—teeth? Have you a cavity?"

"I might, I suppose. Though nothing hurts at the moment."

How It Works

Though Angie and Leon have just married, and though she has scheduled a strictly-business lunch with her ex, Leon's anger helps her choose a sure way to calm him down.

"I said I had to wash my hair."

"You didn't say when."

"This is a hell of a time to lay bath tile."

Wrapped in light-blue terry cloth, Angie glared down at her husband of three weeks. Facing her, pads strapped to his knees, Leon was cold-chiseling grout, tap-tapping with a hammer. Broken tiles surrounded him. A carton of new ones, a sack of Permabond, and two buckets—one half-filled with water—waited in the tub beside him.

"Thought I'd try to finish before the upstairs gets too hot." With a rag he wiped sweat from his bald head.

Angie was ten years younger and, like him, once divorced. They'd met in AA, dated for six months before making love, phoned their sponsors, as instructed, every morning. This new marriage increasingly felt right. But last week she'd set up a lunch with her ex, hoping to decide amicably how much rent to ask for the loft the ex and she owned together. They had lived in it for several years.

Angie's sponsor had urged her to sell; so had Leon. "Stop playing with fire," her sponsor had said.

If Leon pulled in sufficient royalties on the nonfictional *Santa Fe Exposé* his agent had just sold to Viking—or if Angie could find a gallery to show her no-holds-barred oils of paired nudes—maybe she would sell.

Leon and she did aim someday to buy this two-story tumbledown they'd rented southwest of town.

Angie massaged the flaps of terry cloth covering her breasts. "I'm feeling anxious, Leon. It's almost eleven."

"Can't you use the guest shower downstairs?"

"I could but I'm thinking you're hogging our bathroom to spite me."

"Why would I do that?" He lay the hammer down, straightened his back, and placed his palms on his thighs.

"Obvious."

"Well, it is a bit of a triangle, isn't it?"

"You know I don't love him."

"Doll, I don't know squat."

"After last night?"

"Last night was good."

"Well?"

"Our sex is good."

"That's it?"

"You know what your sponsor said."

Angie sniffed.

"Stop playing footsie with a guy who kept cheating on a beautiful woman." Leon aimed his forefinger at her.

"And hit me."

"Doll? You and I got into the fellowship, we endure Al-Anon, both of us try to detach with love. Go ahead, have your fucking lunch. In any case, you can't get the floor wet for twenty-four hours after I screed adhesive to the new tiles and tap them into place. Which I'm about to do. And, okay, I owe you a Tenth Step: I was pissed. Am pissed. Am trying to make it none of my business."

He picked up a wire brush, scrubbed the exposed concrete clean, wiped it with the rag. As he pushed back the shower doors to reach for the Permabond and half-filled bucket, Angie said, "Leon?"

"Yeah?"

"Will you make love to me again?"

"Now?"

"I'm not going to meet him."

"Can you call?"

"He used to hit me, Leon."

"So you're just going to let him show up?"

"And enjoy his margarita. By the third round he won't even remember why he's there."

Renegade

Thriving in routine, fifty-year-old bachelor twins Ronnie and Ralph never vary what they eat, so when Ralph suggests substituting beans for soup for fun, Ronnie lashes out.

Ralph's and Ronnie's new boss at the state's Educator Ethics Bureau—this time a woman—called them Tweedledum and Tweedledee behind their backs, though the twins couldn't have looked less similar. Ralph was skinny and short, and his skin was clear. His high voice seemed a woman's. The mustachioed Ronnie was pudgy and short. Moles marred his face. His gravelly bass tagged him as a smoker, though he'd never been one.

Only in their eating habits did the middle-aged bachelors seem twins. Dinner proceeded as follows:

Ralph prepared appetizers, four ham and turkey slices rolled tight, each end dabbed in organic mayonnaise. The brothers nibbled these while watching the news. Afterward, Ronnie divided a can's worth of heart-healthy soup into bowls, covered them with saran, punctured the wrap, and microwaved the result.

When their spoons could scoop up no more, they used their forefingers to lick the bowls clean, starting at the top and spiraling down.

Ralph set dessert—two cubes of ginger and three chocolate kisses—on smoky-glass plates that had been their mother's.

Later they settled on the sofa to watch a film noir from Netflix while chewing a cleansing lump of spearmint gum.

Once a month their new boss treated them to lunch at Saveur across the street. They filled their plates with asparagus, salmon, couscous, and salad, adding sunflower seeds. Both drank their coffee black.

After five months, their boss said, "You fellas always seem to order the same damn meal. Don't you ever get sick of doing that?"

"Never." The pudgy twin, Ronnie, smoothed his mustache, starting the mole on his nose to tickle.

"We never vary, Vivian," the skinny twin, Ralph, added in his soprano. "Kinda strange, you bet."

"Not strange at all," Ronnie said. "Keeps life simple."

That evening while preparing appetizers, Ralph said, "Ronnie? Know what? Viv might be right. About being in a rut. Been chewing it over. We're gonna turn fifty. The next time she treats, instead of fixing soup for dinner, let's try beans from a can. Couldn't be simpler."

"No way, bro."

"As an experiment. See how we feel."

"I'd rather forget the news than change our diet, granola and yogurt for breakfast, egg sandwiches at our desks, the dinners we do. Keeps us fit."

"But I'm sick of it, Ronnie. I never realized—"

"Don't realize. Remember that I'm five minutes older. Without me, bro, you're nothing."

Ralph slammed the plate of appetizers onto the counter. "That hurts, Ronnie. It sure does. Now you guess what. Before Mother passed, she told me she had always and forever loved me the best."

Gone

To Harold, wife Stella is becoming a pain in the ass until he hits on a scheme to convince her she's losing her marbles, but who turns out the loser?

Stella's driving the Lexus home this morning with more water-thirsty flowers to plant—cosmos, petunias, snapdragons, marigolds, zinnias, and those huge, in-your-face African daisies—was a last straw for Harold.

He knew she'd bought this latest extravagance simply to remind her of their garden in smoggy Sacramento before he had cajoled her—*cajoled* being her word—to flee to sun-drenched Santa Fe, so that finally, in a sea of art, she could set sail to become a painter, ending a decades-long whine about not having the right ambience to get started.

Goddamn it, the decision to move here had been jointly made! Two years ago they'd sunk nearly a million bucks into purchasing mortgage-free this eye-popping hacienda with its separate, nearly-all-glass studio. Canyon Road galleries bloomed with art half a block away, painters and sculptors paraded their Cavalier King Charles toy spaniels and Llasa apsos up and down, back and forth, and what did Stella plunge into doing? Gardening. Xeric? Oh, no. She'd even converted the studio into a greenhouse for cymbidiums.

Lately she'd been complaining about having no grandchildren. How can you have grandchildren if you don't have children?

While Harold played poker on the Internet and watchdogged their tax-free bonds, his Pookie was becoming an increasing pain in the ass, and he had begun hanging out at Downtown Subscription coffeehouse, hoping to meet a woman willing, at least in public, to refrain from bellyaching.

He watched Stella now from the window of his den unload flat after cardboard flat of little green pots, and found himself yearning to drive this wife of thirty-odd years as bonkers as she was driving him—drive her out of his life, when a plan like an angel descended.

Fast-forward a week: before the sun rose on Tuesday, he rolled toward Stella in bed, kissed her earlobe, tiptoed to the hall closet where he'd stowed jacket, shirt, jeans, and boots, and slipped out to the yard where flowers and sprigs of greenery bordered stepping stones leading to the front gate.

Each morning thereafter he yanked up every third plant and smoothed each hole's walls with a trowel. When Stella saw the damage, he explained,

"Pookie, look, that's obviously not the work of an animal. Somebody has got it in for you. Did you offend anyone yesterday?"

She replanted, of course, but when the uprootings continued, she asked him to call the police. He delayed until she screamed bloody murder. When two cops came, he and Stella gave their report, and the plants kept vanishing. Harold began taking an extra fifteen minutes to pull snaps and zinnias from one side of a picket fence Stella had stripped the polyurethane from and painted white.

By the middle of June she'd decided—after consulting friends from Sacramento who had left for the Rossmoor Adult Community in Walnut Creek—that that's where she was heading, with Harold or not.

"Don't know we can afford it, Pookie." But windfalls from real estate investment trusts made him suspect that, by taking out a mortgage, he could purchase a second home.

Stella had left before September arrived, though many of her pantsuits with their scent of talcum still hung in the bedroom's walk-in closet. Several times he had resolved to cart them to the Salvation Army depot off Cerrillos but couldn't bring himself to act. He'd thrown out the cymbidiums, though, and, to maintain property value, hired a woman bent by osteoporosis to keep the garden up.

Three, four times a week he'd stroll the two blocks to Downtown Subscription for a chicken-salad burrito and bottle of carbonated pear nectar, sit and gawk or read *Barrons*, and wonder why was it so damnably hard to make friends.

Sand

Harold, remembering his love for sand as a child, builds and tests out a sandbox indoors for his grandson, but receives from the boy a surprise response.

"You've done what?" Harold's daughter asked.

Harold lowered the receiver to his thigh and gazed at his secret gift—two weeks in the making—waiting in the living-room's near corner for his grandson's visit.

He'd laid an oversized polyethylene sheet on the apartment's carpeting; secured four two-by-twelves with electrical tape and roofing nails inside and out at each corner, painting them red; and had dragged twenty-seven, fifty-pound bags of sand from the drive where the truck had dumped them.

"One of the bags broke in the outside hallway," Harold said, receiver up close to his lips again. "Musta taken an hour to get that hall runner clean, but I had to—the manager makes his monthly run tomorrow."

"And what's he going to say when he sees your sandbox?"

"It's not mine, Jill. It's Mac's, for his eighth birthday. Whenever he wants. Though I may test it out."

"What's the manager going to say, Dad?"

"He never comes in."

"And if someone tells him?"

"Who?"

"How the hell should I know? Eight seems kinda old for a sandbox, anyway, doesn't it?"

"You'll feel better when you get here, honey. I've stashed a camouflage tarp in the closet for the times Mac's not here."

"Ugly."

"Think whoopee. See you in what, twenty minutes? Don't forget the key I gave you."

"You watched me put it on my chain."

"Don't forget his trucks, then. I've bought blocks and a pail and scooper."

Harold had never had a sandbox. Growing up at the beach in southern California meant all the sand for tunnels and forts he'd needed. Too bad Santa Fe had no kelp for atmosphere, let alone ocean to hear.

Yup, best do a test run.

As he stripped off sneakers and socks, corduroys, tartan shirt, and tee,

Harold's mind suggested this was nutso. His knee joints stung when he rose from a chair. His razor missed whole clumps of whiskers.

But the bird of caution went bye-bye. Wincing, the pint-size septuagenarian managed to crouch and suddenly realized that Mac would need water to build roads and a castle. But oh, this brought good memories. He grabbed up sand and watched it trickle out, sparkling under the ceiling light he'd snapped on to simulate the sun. He shifted to his side and wriggled in the grains, smiling to feel them prick his hip and shoulder, work into the elastic of his drawers as they once did swimming trunks.

When his daughter knocked, he was busy squirming on his back attempting to make an angel in sand. "Come on in," he yelped.

Mac preceded his mother in jeans that dragged on the rug and a collared, short-sleeve top.

"Happy birthday, McAllister."

"What are you doing down there, Grandad?"

Harold rolled onto a bony buttock and spread his arms. "It's all yours, Mac."

"All my what?"

Harold's daughter followed Mac in, cradling her purse and an armful of toys: dump truck, flatbed, front loader painted yellow, a Caterpillar, a pickup. When she saw her father nearly naked, her lips sprang wide.

"All your what?" Harold said, repeating Mac's question. "All this sand."

"Wheezo jeezo, Grandad. Get a grip, huh?"

Wants More

Not Martin's lackluster in bed but his refusal to leave Santa Fe prompts his woman to wonder what to do.

"What are you doing on your knees?"

"Praying for a customer."

"Can I help?"

"Scrubb floors elsewhere."

"That was mean!"

"I mean if nobody opens that door."

"This was a crazy idea, anyway, Martin."

"Moving to Santa Fe?"

"Opening a used-childrens'-clothing store."

"You said you wanted kids."

"C'mon. Ours."

"I'm too old."

"That's why you can't get it up?"

"Now who's mean?"

"It's dark down here on the floor. But look what I found—an unused stamp."

"Better'n nothing. I oughta go freshen the window display."

"Martin?"

"My knees hurt."

"Hold me."

"For a moment."

"You're a good man, baby."

"Except in bed?"

"Martin? I know what the trouble is."

"No customers."

"Effluvium from Los Alamos. Chem trails. Arsenic in the water. Exhaust. Let's leave this high-desert hellhole."

"But we've made friends—I love it here. Where are you going?"

"Out."

"Of my life?"

"I'm not sure."

Engagement

College-student Aaron wonders what the gorgeous young woman his father is engaged to has up her sleeve, and why give Aaron that come-hither look?

The college's cafeteria swarmed with students chattering under the skylights, but student Aaron Ruhenstein remained in shock. The girl that his father had brought out from New Jersey couldn't be much older than Aaron himself.

He sat across from Hannah, trying to keep his eyes off the gold Star-of-David pendant that brushed first one side of her cleavage, then the other, as she cut bits from the quarter-breast of chicken and its attached leg.

No fucking fair, Dad, no fair.

Unlike his son or Hannah, Jay Ruhenstein had lifted the plate of chicken and veggies, lettuce and sprouts and pearl tomatoes, his brownie and coffee off his tray, and set it aside. Nothing had spilled.

Grapefruit juice lay pooled in the corner of Aaron's.

"Takes me back," Jay said, picking gristle from between his teeth with a pinkie's glistening nail. "Chums breaking bread together—although at Yale each college had its own dining hall. Are you making friends yet, Aaron? We had to drive to Radcliffe or Smith for our gals but no need for that here."

"Oh!" Hannah's fork had dropped to the floor. She hunched her shoulders and smiled across at Aaron, launching him to his feet. An unlaced high-top squeaked as he headed for the salad bar's utensil dispenser.

I've made friends in our Muslims-for-Peace group, Dad, but you wouldn't want to know about that.

She accepted the clean fork, speared a couple of overcooked string beans, and inserted them between unglossed lips.

"Feast your peepers on this baby, boy kid." Jay lifted Hannah's wrist to show off her finger's platinum band. It supported a diamond lozenge and chips of sapphire.

"It's too big, don't you think?" Hannah said.

Aaron's forehead, bumpy from last year's high-school acne, grew hot. "You're asking me?"

She nodded.

"Oh, this bubelah," Jay said. "Everything I do she says it's too much. I swore to your mother I'd never remarry but here's Miss Gorgeous ushering at

City Ballet and you know what a dance goofball I am. She wants to put our money to work building health clinics on the West Bank."

Our money, Aaron wondered? Did Hannah wink at him? Some kind of do-gooder gold digger? True, he could not see himself working for his dad other than summers in the apron-manufacturing business his granddad had founded. But he hated to see his former-star-fullback father taken.

You bitch.

Jay, at the end of the table, and Aaron watched Hannah attempt to separate the chicken leg from its quarter breast with knife and fork—until her frustrated pout caused the boy to blurt, "Grab hold of the end of the bone."

She locked her black eyes on his, then did as she was told.

Aaron reached over the napkin holder, took away her knife, and sawed the sinew in two.

But when Aaron looked up she had shifted her gaze towards his father, the usually-smooth brow of the bullet head creased deeper than he'd ever seen.

Bonding

After emotionally-challenged Genevieve invites new-friend Pam to share the dessert that Genevieve's dead daughter most loved, Pam recoils at Genevieve's sudden slap.

Genevieve brushed fingertips across the cilantro she'd been nurturing. Its stems and leaves wove like green plumes from the box she'd set on the rotting sill facing south in her apartment. Most afternoons the sun lit both the herb and the railroad tracks below.

Pam, a new friend she'd met in the college cafeteria, was due any moment off the bus for a midafternoon treat. The college's director of human resources had bargained with the manager of the food concession to give Genevieve, Pam, and a few other emotionally-challenged Santa Feans free breakfasts, lunches, and dinners in exchange for an hour of weeding or, when the weather grew raw, sweeping and dusting classrooms.

For Genevieve, the cilantro's fans of pink and white spoke of hope, in contrast to the dark-brown sofa and dining table, the scarred lamps, the warped chest that held her daughter's trousseau—she'd died in a train wreck days before her wedding.

Maggie had loved praline-crunch ice cream, which Genevieve meant to serve Pam today, and as a young woman, Maggie had grown to crave her mother's cilantro, baby lettuce, pecan, and carrot-sliver salad. But this Genevieve had refused to fix ever since Maggie's burial.

The buzzer sounded and Genevieve lumbered to the door, opening it to a woman half her weight.

"Hello, hello, hello." Genevieve adjusted the fringed scarf she'd wrapped around thinning hair. After breakfast she'd stolen a rose from the dozen brightening the college's coffee bar. It now lay tucked behind one ear.

"Hello yourself, Gen."

"C'mon in."

The shoulder pads in the hollyhock-flowered dress Pam had bought at the Salvation Army seemed to Genevieve like budding wings.

"Love, love, love those white galoshes, gal," she said, leading the taller woman by the elbow toward the sofa. "You think they might be what angels wear when their clouds clog with rain?"

A laugh broke from Pam's flat chest. "You've got some mind. Oh, stop, Gen. Is that cilantro there?"

"From seed."

"Mama grew cilantro, rosemary, basil, dill, chives—you won't believe this. I used to sprinkle torn-up cilantro over vanilla ice cream."

"I'm serving us praline-crunch with Oreos."

"Well, mercy." Pam ran to the window and started plucking the cilantro's leaves, layering them in her palm.

The rose tumbled from Genevieve's ear as she hurried over and whacked Pam's cheek. "What're you thinking, what, what, entering a new friend's home and laying it to waste?"

Hunching her shoulders, Pam backed away, pressing her cheek's stinging flesh. An artery pulsed in her temple. "I wanted to show gratitude, is all. Here." Pam opened her fist. "For you."

"For you, you mean."

"For us."

"Are you leaving?"

"You slapped me."

"Don't go. Slap *me*."

Instead, galoshes squeaking, Pam walked to one of the settings at the table and slapped the mat.

Cilantro on praline crunch? Yucch. But Genevieve thanked Pam for being so generous, nibbled a bit of Oreo, sat down beside her friend, and dug in.

Double Vision

After three bum marriages, Glenn's live-in daughter wants to leave Santa Fe for a retirement community where Glenn's parents had lived, but Glenn has good reason to balk.

*B*ecause Glenn's only child, Miranda, had been divorced three times in Santa Fe, she got itchy to replant the two of them in Southern California, where Glenn and her mother had raised her. "Laguna Beach, Dad! Warm winters! I can paint there just as well. High-octane gallery scene. You taught me how to surf just twenty miles north, remember?

"Laguna Beach, Miranda? That's plunging down the on ramp. Prices must be worse than here. Where we're happy housekeeping together, aren't we?"

"Then what about Golden Oaks?"

He stiffened. "You're not old enough."

"I could dye my hair all-the-way gray."

Glenn's parents had lived out their lives in Golden Oaks, seven clubhouses on two thousand acres ten minutes inland from Laguna Beach.

"Tell you a secret." Miranda brought over a plate of turkey bacon and scrambled egg whites. "I sent for a DVD."

"Of the beach?"

"Of Golden Oaks. That time we flew out to visit your folks? So many trees in blossom! Walking paths, cottontails, you could almost hear the ocean. I need a change, Dad, I really do. Too many bum marriages in Santa Fe." She bent to hug his neck from behind.

"Can't hurt to look, I guess."

She pulled the shades, scrunched close to him on the sofa, and thumbed the remote. The camera swept Golden Oaks' homes and apartments from above, then surveyed interiors, clubhouses, the creek, two golf courses, the tennis courts surrounded by jacarandas blooming, lawn-bowling greens, horse trails.

"Oh, Dad, it's gorgeous!"

But Glenn felt sick. Instead of what the screen showed, all he could see were imges formed from his sister's phone calls that he thought, through therapy, he'd put to rest.

His own ghost camera showed his mother hunched in the guest room, clutching his sister's baby daughter, dead from a grand mal. It showed his father raging at his sister's husband the following spring, cuffing his ear, backhanding his scotch, sending glass and ice smashing into a photo of Glenn and his sister. Who later had taken her life by overdosing on antidepressants.

"Can't do it," Glenn whispered.

"What, Dad?"

"Leave."

"Why?"

"The sorrows. They're all still there."

Perplexed

The young woodworker that Sarah has taken for her latest live-in lover bristles at what she intends as constructive criticism.

"What's the matter?" Sarah, a wealthy widow from Saint Louis, brushed her palm down Cal's neck.

"I'm brooding," he said.

"So I can see." She pushed a shock of chestnut hair off his forehead. Older than Cal by fourteen years, having lived with a string of men following her husband's death, Sarah owned the gallery that formed the first floor of her home off Camino Escondido.

They sat catercorner at the dinette table Cal had fashioned from cherrywood in the shop at Santa Fe Community College.

Last year he had arrived from Fort Wayne during Santa Fe's construction boom, to earn money as a carpenter while pursuing his passion as a furniture maker, at the same time earning an Associate's Degree in Applied Arts.

Sarah, who taught a course in watercolors on campus, upon learning that Cal slept in his car, proposed he come live with her and give up home-building.

You know, Cal," she said, caressing the table, "I'd like to see you add brass caps. Will you do that? You see how the corners are scuffing?"

"You asked me what's the matter. What's the matter is that with you nothing's ever right."

"Oh, now." She forked up the last of the huevos rancheros he'd cooked. He watched the folds of her neck rise as she finished her coffee.

"Would you mind?" She handed him her mug.

He refilled it from the stove.

"Did you treat your other men this way?" he asked, returning.

How do you mean, darling?"

"Like a robot that's been miswired."

"Very nice, Cal. And so untrue. A kiss?"

He lipped her cheek. "I don't even measure up in bed. Did the others need to diddle you off?"

"I won't listen to this! You see now how *I'm* sulking?" She hopped her chair backwards and stood. "And we planned to take a walk this gorgeous morning."

"I like doing things together, Sarah. I like making things for you. But you always undercut. Last night I thought I was giving you pleasure but you had to tell me, 'Oh, Cal, your pelvis, it's so bony, am I not feeding you right? Darling, tell me what to buy, we need to give you some padding down there.'"

"All right, I'm crying now. Happy?"

Cal finished off his papaya nectar. "Every day I thank God that you give me money to get an education, that you want to show my chairs and cabinets and side tables downstairs with your paintings. But I'm too thin. And you probably wish I were taller. And you think my cherrywood table needs decorative corners." He scratched a forearm tattooed with the word *Mom* inscribed in a heart. "What in hell is it that you want from me, anyway?"

"What do I want? Simple." She pulled a lavender hankie from her robe. "Your presence, Cal."

Loneliness

Rudy and Coral, meeting in a poetry-writing group, discover they like each other even though dealing with global warming in different ways.

Rudy and Coral had just joined, independently, a long-established poetry-writing group that met at Harry's Roadhouse Thursday afternoons. Rudy immediately took to Coral's horsy scent, whisking him back to childhood riding lessons his parents had treated him to.

During the group's ten minutes of let's-say-who-we-are, Rudy had learned that Coral and he had grown up in rural New Hampshire. He also heard her call global warming *a planetary thing.*

At the break, she'd invited him to drive out to Cerrillos sometime, meet her chickens and the two mares.

After the poetry session ended, Rudy and Coral lingered near the newspaper-vending machines that lined the way to the parking lot. Rudy flipped his dark glasses down to soften the sun's glint, and stared at the still-narrow-waisted woman with hooked nose and close-set eyes he thought he might ask out for dinner following the group's next get-together. First, however, he wanted to hear more of her views on global warming.

"We simply need to accept and adapt," she told him. "It's how I've lived my life since my daughter ended hers."

"My lord! How?"

She lowered the brim of a hat enlivened by straw cornflowers. "Borrowed her boyfriend's shotgun."

"But why?"

"She found me unfeeling. He sold meth for a living. Long ago." Coral narrowed her eyes. "Now I play."

"You were a lawyer."

"And you told us you were a physics professor."

"Too many migraines discovering that all proven conclusions are temporary," Rudy said. "Supervising grounds maintenance at Los Alamos suits me better."

"United States capitol of pit production."

"Like you, I try to accept and adapt. Though my digestion's worsening knowing that we're courting inevitable cataclysm, whether nature's or our own making. Or both."

"Your climate poems upset several of the group."

"Not you?"

"Easier on my nerves to call global warming nature's busywork, Rudy. Okay, maybe I'm too much like the head of Iran, denying the Holocaust. Or that fourteenth-century Spaniard who disbelieved the world a globe; the born-again Christian who can't comprehend how suicide bombers are so sure they're blowing themselves into the arms of Allah."

"I'm a bit lost."

"Come see my horses?" She placed her palm on his forearm.

He started shifting his feet.

"Do I scare you? A lawyer yet so illogical? Ponder this. We can choose whatever belief system makes us happiest. After Amy pulled the trigger, I discarded cause and effect. Which means I needn't believe in time—even physicists say it's unreal, right? I do wish you'd come out and visit me. Suppose time does exist. Both of us doubt there's much of it left. And you and I have lots in common, starting with the wrinkles in our necks."

Just Do It

Of the three sixth-grade friends, Rodney learns soonest that smoking crushed dock seeds isn't the only reason for violence.

Mr. Freeback owned two adobe outbuildings near his back fence. One stored his tractor, one gardening tools and pots. The alley the structures formed had become shady headquarters for the Agua Fria Bums: Rodney, Alejandro, and Sean. They gathered afternoons to discuss how they'd like to undress certain sixth-grade girls and what they'd like to do next.

Today was their first to crush and smoke the winged seeds of curly dock, as instructed by a gang of seventh graders who'd graduated to tobacco from what they called monkey shit. The dock grew five feet high on the far side of the tractor garage, out of sight from Freeback's house. The Bums had allowed Rodney's sister, Gardenia-Rose, to place scissors and a page Rodney tore the night before from the family Bible under a boulder beside the garage—then to scram.

Unknown to the other Bums or Gardenia-Rose, Rodney was saving up to fly her and himself to Colorado's Canyon City to visit their mother, imprisoned a year ago for dealing crack. That's why the boy accepted ten dollars on Tuesdays, and another ten on Fridays, from Uncle Oscar, his and Gardenia-Rose's caretaker.

This Friday, Uncle Oscar had not used enough Vaseline, though Rodney had agreed to bend over far enough to grab his ankles, rather than, as usual, flattening his chest against the mattress. As he limped across the lot that bordered Freeback's outbuildings, his anus stung as though sliced.

When he reached headquarters, he accidentally kicked over a can of Coke and before he could right it, a whiptail lizard had sped from under the boulder to lap the liquid up. While Alejandro scissored the page from Holy Writ, Sean gathered dock seeds and crushed them. Each boy rolled their monkey shit and twisted shut the ends of what used to form part of Chapter Four from *Leviticus.*

But after finishing his cigarette, Rodney barfed near a stack of windows Mr. Freeback had leaned against the garden-tool outbuilding's wall. He lurched to the side as Alejandro let his own mess flow. The vomit soaked one of Sean's boots and Sean whopped Alejandro's shoulder, sending him sprawling.

Rodney stepped over the fallen Alejandro and launched his sneaker into Freeback's windows, over and over until blood drenched his sock.

Slogging Through It

W. Dan Quattlebaum reminds fourth-grade teacher Adele of her stoop-shouldered, now-dead father, which is why she hopes he'll lunch with her after entertaining the class with his birdsong imitations.

"Children, this is the biology surprise I talked about yesterday, Mister W. Dan Quattlebaum."

A stoop-shouldered man in a cardigan, hair falling past flaring ears, left the chair that the fourth-grade teacher, Miss Adela Cunningham, had placed next to her desk, and bowed.

"Mr. Quattlebaum will show us blow-ups of winter birds common in Santa Fe. He'll also be imitating their calls."

"And thongs, ma'am."

"And songs. So that even if you can't see the bird, you can brag to your parents, sister, brother, or best friend that you know what that bird is."

A hand shot up.

"Albert?"

"Is this also to help us keep from getting pooped on?"

Two girls tittered and Ralph at the next desk slapped the collar of Albert's jacket.

"I won't bother answering that. You're all to take notes and hand in a two-page report Thursday, double-spaced as always. Our first bird, Mr. Quattlebaum?"

The old man tilted a slight chin and swallowed, causing his Adam's apple to rise. What Adela saw, however, was her beloved daddy propped against the hospital pillow last fall, trying to strengthen his breathing by blowing air into a tube, causing a yellow ball to rise.

W. Dan launched into a series of short, low-pitched whistles, speeding them up near the end. His shoulders shook with each whistle.

"Any guethes?" he asked, stretching a plaid bow tie from his throat and letting it snap back.

Ralph raised his hand. "You've just seen a good-looking honey?"

"That'll do," Adela said. "Mr. Quattlebaum, what—" She thought she'd finished with the crying jags but the stinging started again. She turned toward the blackboard, clenched her teeth until they hurt, snuffled, extracted a tissue from her pocket, and faced forward. "Class? What bird have we just heard?"

W. Dan hauled up one of the matted photos wedged between his chair and the desk, and held it toward the students.

"Owl?" a girl asked.

He rested the photo against the leg of his checkered slacks. "Wethtern screech owl. The male hath a lower voice than hith mate."

Several boys fisted their giggles.

"Next, Mr. Quattlebaum?"

"Thong," he said and pursed his lips. "Teewee, teewee, teewee." He repeated the sequence, then said, "Call: thikadee-dee. Thikadee-dee-dee."

"Chickadee!" a girl yelped.

"Nope."

Nope—Daddy's word. Even when I put my cheek to his and whispered, "I love you," he shrugged and stared up at the heat vent and then died. Mother stayed away. At least her boyfriend loves her.

W. Dan rummaged among the photos, brought one up, and displayed it. "Thee the topknot? Plain titmouth. Gray all over. Hangth upthide down on feederth."

"Mr. Quattlebaum?

"Yeth?"

"Before you demonstrate our third call—"

"And thong."

"And thong—song. Will you let me buy you lunch at Saveur? Something nice for all your trouble this morning?"

"Been no trouble."

"Will you let me? Albert, Ralph, back in your chairs. We don't throw gliders in the classroom."

"But mine has a message for Stephanie."

"I don't care!"

"I'd be honored," W. Dan said.

Wacko

Diana's lover has been stealing art supplies from her shop, planning to become her rival, prompting Diana—upset now with her waiter—to claim everyone in Santa Fe is wacko.

Diana, who owned a framing shop, and Charlotte, painter of cloudscapes, sat facing each other against the wall of La Chamisa Lunchroom, deciding what to order.

The menus lay open but Diana, because she was crying, couldn't read.

Charlotte pulled a tissue from her purse.

"It hurts. A lot." Diana blotted her eyes. "More than that, it's been making me grind my teeth and now one's loose and this afternoon it may need pulling."

"But you and David were so tight, we all thought in a month we'd be seeing a ring."

"The creep, oh, the lousy..."

"He actually thought you wouldn't confront him?" Charlotte asked.

"Ladies?" A wispy-haired waiter sidled up. Like the other waiters he wore a black bow tie. "More time?"

Charlotte nodded while Diana averted her eyes toward a gaggle of ceramic geese ascending a near wall.

"David was stealing sheets of your non-glare glass?"

"Slowly, so I wouldn't notice. Not just the glass. He took my birch, maple, ash, and ebony molding, even rolls of wire and the kraft backing."

"To set up in competition? But that's—"

Diana, still facing the wall, thrust her palm behind her as though pushing away reality. "Crazy? Don't say it. *I'm* the fool."

Charlotte began to laugh and snatched up her linen napkin. "I'm sorry, dear heart, but it's such a good story."

The aging waiter returned. "Are we ready?"

"I think maybe."

"No."

"May I help?" he asked Diana.

"Give me a moment."

"Of course, sweetheart."

"She's your sweetheart?" Charlotte cleared her throat. "Put me down for the spinach omelet, a side salad, and mint tea."

He lipped a toothbrush mustache and started scribbling.

Diana balled up Charlotte's tissue and gazed through the mist at the menu.

"Our special today is red-chile-dusted calamari, flash fried," the waiter said.

"Yucch."

"You might actually like it."

"You're wrong."

"Of course. Perhaps the sweet potato blintz?"

"Bite your tongue a minute, can you?"

"Of course."

"Haven't you something easy on the stomach?"

"Sweet potato blintz."

"I don't want sweet potato blintz."

"Of course."

"Quit saying that!"

The waiter lipped his mustache.

"Give me a bowl of the cream of squash, a slice of bread, and the same tea my friend's having."

"That would be mint."

"Good for you—I'm sorry."

The waiter bowed and left toward the kitchen's swinging doors.

"You know something?" Diana said. "I can't stand this place anymore."

"La Chamisa?"

"Santa Fe. Everyone here's wacko, including me."

Charlotte placed her hand on her friend's fist. "But Diana, *sweetheart*"—she lowered her voice to mimic the waiter's—"that's why we stay."

On the Mend

In the vegan café, Benjamin, long gaga over a white-haired woman he doesn't know, starts talking with a waitress—younger—whose tattoo reads, "What gets in the way is the way."

Kali, *mothering murderess...*
This was the Tuesday that a young PhD from New Mexico Tech had determined to speak to the woman he felt might be his anima.

Deep into studying Jung, he'd set for next week his first visit with a Jungian therapist, hoping to find how he, Benjamin, should be spending his time—in addition to making calls helping housewives disentangle their computers' electronic snarls.

Now he hopped from his Subaru and strode toward Good-Karma Cuisine, a vegan café where increasingly he ate lunch.

Increasingly because often the woman sat in a far corner, a fine-boned, middle-aged goddess whom he called Kali. Her whitening hair streamed to her waist, secured on top by the face of Siva worked in silver. Or was it the arch-demon, Raktavija? She sipped her hibiscus or perhaps ylang-ylang tea and gazed with blue eyes into his own brown whenever he brought his bowl of kitchari to a table nearby.

A garland of skulls dangled from her left wrist. He had to will his hand to stop shaking when he lifted his spoon.

Fifteen minutes earlier than was his habit, he opened the door fashioned from black bamboo and, as he'd hoped, saw that her table so far was empty. *Join me, won't you? We need to talk.* He'd practiced last night in front of his closet's mirror.

Though what if this morning she'd learned of an offspring's death or been rear-ended, and didn't appear at all?

"You seem sad," said the curly-haired girl at the counter, backdropped by canisters of teas, beans, and spices.

"Does the white-haired woman who sits there in the corner lunch here every day?"

"Just about...what about you? Want your usual?"

Benjamin nodded. He hadn't much noticed the girl before. He liked her scent of sandalwood. "Hold still," he said.

"Why?"

"I want to read your tattoo."

She turned a freckled shoulder toward him. *What gets in the way is the way* wound down in red toward her elbow.

"Food for thought," Benjamin said.

She ladled mung beans, carrots, broccoli, and bok choy over steaming rice, sprinkled on ginger, and placed the bowl on a lacquered tray, then poured him a cup of black tea, lightened it with soy milk, and spooned in turbinado sugar.

"I've never watched you work before," he said.

"Does it lift your mood?"

He smiled yes and carried his tray to the table.

Ten minutes later the goddess had not showed up. He nudged his bowl aside and, cheeks in palms, watched the girl retrieve empty dishes from other tables—such a spring to her step.

His cell phone chimed. To the housewife in cyberspace distress he lamented that the afternoon was filled but that tomorrow he'd be there early.

His head felt like a tombstone and the last of his tea tasted bitter.

"Okay if I sit?" a voice asked behind him.

It was the girl's. He pulled out a chair, noticing that a bearded boy now stood behind the register.

"I wonder where your friend is."

"Yeah," Benjamin mourned.

"You've fallen in love with her?"

"You've noticed?

"You always sit near each other but neither of you speak. What's the story?"

"There is none yet."

"I'm Julie."

They began to talk, sharing for nearly half an hour—where they'd gone to college, how they'd ended up in Santa Fe, what they liked here, what they hated—when the bamboo door swung in and Kali appeared.

Benjamin saw her glance at them as she floated toward the counter.

"Shall I go?" Julie asked.

"Don't you have to?"

"I've got ten minutes. But you told me you'd finally screwed up your courage to introduce yourself to her."

"Stay, okay?" He gripped the arm of her chair. "What gets in the way is the way."

Distraction

Roxanne's hip hurts bad but this pain, she tells Bruce, is nothing compared to the week she'll soon have to endure his daughter, who's told him, "Any love you have for me sucks."

"Sarah Palin."

"Running for president?"

"Run for your life."

"Sarah's failin'."

"Alaskan queen."

"She's palin'."

"How's your hip feel?"

"Hurts like hell, let's keep going."

"Wailin'."

"Exhalin'."

"You're good at this, Rox."

"Ailin'."

"Bailin'."

"Just like me."

Roxanne slithered down her reading pillow until the covers hid all but her nose and eyes and their dark bags. Matted this morning, her hair last week had glowed.

Bruce leaned over. Near their bed, air hot as her forehead rose from the register. Outside, light snow fell.

"I'll make an omelet and bring up some grapefruit juice. Roxanne's prevailin'."

"Derailin'," she said.

"The shot of cortisone tomorrow should help."

"I'll need more than that to deal with your daughter."

"Roxanne's unveilin'."

"Quailin'. Remember Belle's last visit?" Roxanne made her voice huskier. "'Dad, I need to tell you straight. You and Roxanne try, you do. I appreciate your paying for my flight, I do. But you know what? Any love you think you might have for me sucks, I'm sorry, it just doesn't come across.'

"Oh, God, here in two days for a week? At least this time she bought her own ticket. But why does she bother?"

"To make amends?" Bruce said. "She's slogged through her own shit with the stillbirth, and her supposéd fiancé vanishing. Never even caught his name."

"Did she?"

"Know his name?"

"Who the father was."

"That's cruel, Rox."

"I'm exhausted."

"We're availin'."

"Sailin'."

"Railin' against wrong."

"My hero. Bruce?"

"Yeah?"

"We're two amazing dudes, you know that? Oh, babe, I hurt bad."

Hot Box

On a trial separation, Matthew finds he misses domesticity, but when his wife and boys pay a visit, so—unexpectedly—does his girlfriend.

Matthew dropped to his knees when he saw his wife steer the Subaru carrying his sons into the slush by the curb beneath the apartment's Afghan pine.

Higher Power, help us reconcile. I'm begging here, Matthew prayed.

Minutes later, Ella's knock sounded from the hall. He had cleaned the toilet, sponged the tiles, and scented the john with a blast of Plum Blossom. Oatmeal cookies and lemonade sat on the table in the kitchenette. He'd shoved under his mattress the red mitten he'd discovered that Cheyenne, his at-present girlfriend, had left last Sunday between the sofa's arm and back cushion.

"You look great—okay if I hug you?" he asked Ella after opening the door.

She nodded, wearing a bright-colored Pendleton blanket tailored into a coat.

Did he release her too quickly? His therapist had said he was bound to make mistakes. "Hi, boys." His cheeks buzzed as he knelt again and took Christopher's shoulders, then Andy's.

"C'mon in, little family." Too saccharine, he wondered? "I sure do like that outfit, honey."

"Not sure I like this place for you, though, Matthew. It wants curtains." Ella lay the coat across a sofa arm and stretched, tightening the pumpkin-hued sweater over her smallish breasts. A ribbon of the same color pulled her hair off her neck.

"One thing living here has done is given me a few months to think. Boys, pour yourselves some lemonade."

Cheyenne worked the front desk where Matthew left his laundry. If only she'd gone to college, they could converse about more than sex—she relished positions he'd never dreamed possible. Afterward, she liked to smoke and listen to hip-hop, clanking her rings in rhythm against the nearest iron bedpost.

"Honey, thanks for taking the risk." Matthew shifted in his chair so that, per his therapist's suggestion, he faced his wife full on whenever he spoke.

"What risk?" Fingers of the hand that bore her ring twisted her plaid skirt.

Plaid's hokey for Santa Fe, Matthew couldn't help thinking. *Stop judging—the boys need their dad.* "The risk of paying a visit. I miss our talking about the day's happenings, our helping to strengthen each other's manuscripts, our, you know, nights in bed."

"You're the one who left."

"Might you be interested in counseling? Not my therapist, one—"

"What are you getting at, Matthew?"

"I want to come home."

"Do you?"

Why did her harmonics grate on him like electrical wires thrumming?

"Dad, the cookies are gone."

"I'm sure you've both had plenty," Ella said.

Matthew felt himself start to perspire.

From the street came a long honk, followed by two short ones.

But Cheyenne *worked* Thursday mornings.

The honks sounded again.

Matthew jumped up. "Ella, God, I forgot. I'm supposed to meet someone who may want to hire me to help polish her—her biography of the people's historian, Howard Zinn."

He hurried to the window and waved at Cheyenne, crisscrossing his arms as if practicing semaphore. Black hair flowing to her waist, she straddled a chunk of dirty snow between her banged-up Chevy and Ella's Suburu.

Matthew turned. "I'll call you, okay? To set something up. I miss—"

Ella elbowed him aside, went to the window, looked down, and turned. "You sonovabitch."

Sloppy

Jacques Bervier, publicly lauded but never photographed philanthropist, shoplifts groceries to siphon off frustration over three stressors until a youngster calls his bluff.

Financially, Jacques had no need. He owned his Porche outright, purchased vests from Pendleton, loafers and pima cotton shirts from Harry's near the Plaza.

So why shoplift? Three stressors—one, his daughter, citing early abandonment, refused to cash the five-hundred-dollar checks he mailed to Seattle on holidays. Two, so many drivers in Santa Fe ran yellow lights. Three, overpopulation everywhere was shrinking land left for agriculture, requiring a corresponding boost in the use of chemicals, plus the need to transport vegetables and fruits from far away—meaning an unconscionable increase in prices.

Which kept pace with the unconscionable increase in the cost of mood elevators. But never mind that. Today was Thursday.

At last count Santa Fe boasted seventeen food outlets. He figured that by shopping at a different one each week, and marking in a notebook what he wore, then changing his outfit the next week, clerks would not learn to watch for him, and he'd remain free to hone his skills—Jacques Berrier, the publicly lauded but never photographed Good Samaritan who each September gave twenty percent of his adjusted gross income to Food Depot, Kitchen Angels, No More Hungry Tummies, St. Elizabeth Shelter, and, of course, Planned Parenthood, all from bonds bought selling off his father's vineyards.

But he wished he'd not worn a vest this morning. El Labriego Market already felt too warm.

In the queue of carts edging toward the register, Jacques faced a long-braided woman whose derriere seemed two pumpkins, far larger than those pyramided near the sign trumpeting the day's prices. He had lifted produce, packaged goods, and three cloth shopping bags to the conveyor belt. Under the two bags remaining in the cart he'd stashed a couple of Ben & Jerry's Crème Brûlée.

"Hombré!"

The high voice came from behind him. A hand jiggled his cart and someone snapped, "Carlos!"

He twisted back to watch a pock-faced woman pry away the chubby fingers of a boy half Jacques's height. The bottoms of his jeans dragged on the concrete floor.

"I apologize, señor." She grabbed the boy's upper arm and yanked.

"Don't you catch the ice cream under those bags? How come he can do it an' I can't? You gonna slap him, too?" The boy smacked a cheek that as yet needed no razor.

Jacques heard the belt squeak as the pumpkin-assed shopper swung her cart toward the door. He returned his gaze to Carlos's mother, stepmother, aunt, sister, who knew? Licking her upper lip, the bitch dropped her eyes toward his cart. Blood rushed into his forehead. But he said, "These are for you," extracted the sweating pints from beneath the shopping bags, handed them to the boy, pulled his own cart in front of the register, and—eyeing the cashier—pointed to his left. "If you please, add the two ice creams to my bill."

Had he made the smooth move, he wondered?

Mortgages

Lender Geoffry Barlow tells Lilian and Ron—who's just lost his job—that, though a reverse mortgage isn't possible for them, he can offer two other options, one of which is not the end of the world.

Ron and Lilian had met with mortgage broker Geoffrey Barlow ten years ago when they bought their home. Met in this same office on Marcy Street, Barlow spread in the same leather armchair behind the desk, them straight-backed on the same sofa behind the glass-topped coffee table—which this morning held a vase of gladiolas.

In the intervening years Barlow had added anyway forty pounds, grown a squared-off beard, and inserted a gold ring into his left earlobe.

He was summarizing how a reverse mortgage works. "We appraise your home and set up a loan that pays you monthly for, say, thirty years, until the equity in that home runs out. We then allow you to live in the home mortgage-free until you both pass on."

"Can our son inherit it?" Lilian asked.

"Oh, my, yes, to sell or refinance within six months."

"Sounds like a pretty good deal to me," Ron said. "To recap, Geoff, Home Depot closed my assistant-manager slot last week. Lilian and I can't keep up house payments."

"Mr. Barlow knows all that, Ron." She lifted her arm to scratch a spider bite.

"I know he knows. Just wanted to make sure—"

"Making sure's fine and dandy and I *do* know, folks. Life in our twenty-first century's a sorry shame." Barlow turned to his twin monitors. "Let's take another look-see at your financials. Okay." He clicked a couple of keys. "Okay, yeah, good, okay, uh-oh, don't like this."

"Don't like what?" asked Lilian, rising.

Ron grasped her knee and pushed down.

"What are you doing?"

"Stay put, Lily, let's hear Geoff out. I suspect he'll be offering us several options."

"You've got quite a bit of credit-card debt," Barlow murmured.

"Who doesn't?" asked Lilian, resettling on the sofa away from her husband. "Otherwise we couldn't buy groceries." She pinched up a bit of skirt.

"Using three cards?" Barlow made a clucking sound.

"Since 1996," Ron said.

"Happier times, the nineties, but I'm afraid your overall debt-to-equity ratio means no-can-do today. Regarding a reverse, I mean."

Ron leaned to place his hand on the tartan that covered Lilian's thigh. "Other options, Geoff?"

"For...?" asked Barlow.

"Avoiding bankruptcy. We're already down to one car."

"Might your son take over payments until you find another position?"

"He's a gardener," Ron said.

"Ah so. Options. Well..." Barlow bent toward a cabinet of drawers, opened one, straightened, and proffered a snub-nosed .38. "Just kidding—show me a smile, folks. Bankruptcy isn't the end of the world."

Escape

Edwin, rooming at his daughter's though her husband wants him gone, hears coughing underneath the deck and discovers a sleeping-bagged stranger who's come to die.

"*D*ad," Lorraine called down, "if Mark gets back and finds you in those bushes, he's going to bug me again about assisted living. I don't want to hear it—our home is your home now. What are you looking for?"

On hands and knees below the deck, Edwin tilted the bill of his cap. No way he was going to tell her that—basking in his chair this late October afternoon—he thought he'd heard snoring below him. "Dropped my pocket watch, honeypie."

"Mark will think you've gone crackers. I'll help look."

In the gloom, where the hillside leveled out beneath struts supporting the deck, Edwin heard what sounded like a stone knocking another. "No need, Lorraine. Ah, there's the watch," he lied. "I'll just wait to see if I can't spot that Bendire's thrasher that's been singing, then into my room for Mark to find me napping. Nothing for him to bother about."

"He gets concerned."

"He wants me gone, honeypie."

"Oh, Dad."

Edwin heard her close the door from the deck to the guest room, whose corner now displayed his model of the town he'd grown up in, circled by an electric train. He pushed past a yellowing clump of chamisa to peer into the shadows. "Who's there?" he whispered. For sure that looked like the soft end of a sleeping bag.

He crept further in, feeling like an explorer, strangely young.

"'Preciate your holding it right where you are. Got no weapons but I don't smell like roses, either."

The deep, phlegm-filled warble came from near the house wall, where concrete blocks met the embankment.

"Who are you?" Edwin's pupils had widened enough to spot a bald dome rising out of the bag. The collar of a denim jacket surrounded the stranger's neck; side hair streamed past it.

"I tried to keep quiet."

"Sputtering and snuffling?" Edwin asked.

"My grandsons used to laugh before I vamoosed to find someplace more amenable to die in."

"Amenable?"

"Quieter; no one hassling me. Outdoors but sheltered from the rain."

"How long've you been here?"

"Last night." A fit of coughing doubled the stranger over. "I'll be comatose in a few days."

"I'm calling the ambulance."

"'Preciate not. Spent the last half of my life in hospitals. Sprained this, pulled that, opened for gall bladder, opened for colon cancer. Read my book, *Ways to Go*, or back issues of *Mother Jones*—hospitals, sanatoriums, nursing homes, shelters. You'll 'preciate why I decided to hit the road. Don't phone anyone. Or I'll"—he paused to cough and wipe his lips—"find someplace else."

As he wriggled free of his bag, Edwin glimpsed a black, high-topped sneaker covering one foot. The other was bare.

"Your family's going to want to know where you are."

"I left a note not to hunt me down."

"We're supposed to just let you decompose here?"

"'Preciate it."

"This is crazy!" Though Edwin found himself envying the stranger.

"Dad," Lorraine called, "Mark's back."

"Shhh, you'll scare the thrasher. I've found a blind under the deck."

The man began to cough as though he'd swallowed glass. "Sorry," he managed.

Lorraine leaned over the railing. "That didn't sound like you. Are you getting a cold? What's going on down there, Dad?"

"Talking to myself, Lorraine."

"That Mark will believe."

"Tell him I'm adding to my birder's life list and'll be right up."

Where's Mom?

Brothers Tom and Randy get reacquainted while their mother—whom they suspect is hanging their clothes out to dry in back—lies lifeless in the tub.

Time to go. Did she owe her sons an explanation? She wondered how much the older, Tom—adopted at age three—would care.

Dear boys, nothing more I can do. Mom.

She laid the note face up on the bathroom tiles, and lowered herself to the toilet's lid.

Better the bathtub. In case she threw up. She carried over the pitcher of water, Styrofoam cup, the lunch bag holding vials. She'd coaxed prescriptions from four physicians over the past three months.

Tom and Randy said they'd be back in an hour. Should she leave on her panties and bra for decency? Certainly.

Scooting down opposite the spigot, she shivered at the porcelain's chill. She dumped the pink pentagons of Effexor into a fold of her ample tummy, following these with Halcions and the white tabs of Lexapro. For good measure she added half a dozen caps of the antihistamine, Deonamine.

She hoped she didn't pee excessively, though mostly she hoped the transition didn't hurt. She poured her cup full and began to gulp down the pills.

▲▲▲

Son Tom, who ran a pornographic Web site in Oakland, had not seen his brother for a year. Randy had taken over the family's floral shop after his father's death from a ruptured appendix. Having broken off a succession of engagements to marry, Randy had agreed to move back home, though last week he'd warned his mother that he'd be moving out again if she kept hounding him about grandchildren.

"Mom? Randy called, opening the front door. "Come see what Tom bought us." He looked at his brother. "She'll get used to her, Tommy."

In his arms Tom cradled a winged, sitting nude carved from oak, legs stretched straight and spread, nipples raised, arms thrown up, painted lips wide. She seemed flabbergasted at what, having landed, she'd encountered.

"This honey's hot for more," Tom said, fanning out issues of their mother's *Better Homes & Gardens* and setting the half-life-size angel on top. "How about you, bro, what do you do for sex?"

"Use your Web site," Randy said, shutting the front door.

"That's it?"

"I'm pretty busy with work, Tommy."

"Let's go scare us up some nooky tonight."

"I don't know. I've presented the same diamond ring three times, but when it comes to bedding flesh and blood I just go soft."

"You haven't found the right woman, is all."

"Mom fell in love with the last one. It hurt pretty bad to see her cry when I told her the deal was over. How come you never married?"

"No need, buddy," Tom said. "Let's go find out where the old darling is. Probably out back, hanging up our clothes."

"Mom?" Randy shouted. "We're home."

Shopping

Viktor, visiting from New York, finally understands why his old mother is reluctant to hurry their shopping.

Viktor's therapist thought it a fine idea: explain to his mother once again, after so many years, why he had left Santa Fe for New York.

Long ago his father had plucked the three of them *away* from New York and, before he died, become as well-known in Santa Fe as a painter of ikons as Viktor had become known as a television casting agent in the Big Apple.

Had the visit here really been a fine idea? At the Sunport his mother—five foot two to his six foot four—had pried his arms from around her. After breakfast yesterday he'd done all the talking; her tears, which she refused to dry, made her chin hairs shine. She'd wagged her head no to his wanting to kiss her good night, though after he'd slipped under the covers in his old room, she'd opened the door and sat nearby in the dark.

This morning when he'd offered to buy groceries, she'd said, "We go together."

Now, in khakis pressed in New York and a long-sleeved, pima cotton shirt, he guided the cart past a booth selling coffee. She stayed ten feet behind him, wrapped in a brown wool coat that reached her ankles. Bunches of frizzy hair sprang from her scarf.

First stop, apples. He picked up a red Gala and a yellow Delicious and turned. "Mom, which?"

She stared at him.

"Mom?"

She crinkled already-half-shut eyes and pursed her lips.

He tossed the Gala back. "This?" he asked.

She shook her head.

He retrieved the Gala and held it up.

She nodded.

"How many?"

No answer.

Even though he'd be gone in two days, he ripped a couple of see-through bags off the roll and loaded them with Galas.

A growing number of Hispanics, Anglos, Sufis in white turbans, and Native Americans pushed their carts past. A little girl tugged her mother's skirt, gazing as Viktor held up a bunch of spinach. The girl watched the bent, old lady shake her head, watched Viktor hold up some red-stemmed chard, watched the old lady nod, and watched him force two clusters into a bag.

Approaching the locally-baked breads, Viktor consulted his watch. Choosing fruits and veggies had consumed a half hour. Behind him his mother was peering into a refrigerated bin. *She wants cheese? Twenty minutes.*

He brought the cart near, not to shout. "Mom?"

She held up a wedge of Brie, set it back, held up a square of country jack. He grasped her elbow. "Mom, our slow motion is wearing me out."

She raised her shoulders and turned up her palms.

"Do you need bread, cereal, ice cream maybe, milk? I'm getting hungry. Aren't you getting hungry? Let's beat it."

She shook her head.

"No? Why? What's the matter?"

"I'm not going to lose you again."

Probably Not

Though Ella tells her crippled brother she thinks her boss, a truck dealer turned florist, wants to propose, instead he rages because she gets to work a few minutes late.

"I don't think John Henry's the one for you, Ella," said her brother, Nick, from the adjustable barber's chair he sat in to watch Good Morning, America. He used the chair after dinner, too, because of his back. Disability insurance and Ella's job managing John Henry/Flowers paid for renting a rundown, two-bedroom adobe in Santa Fe's South Capitol district.

"He's wants to buy me dinner Saturday, Nick."

"To pop the question?" Nick pulled the lapels of an old, brown robe tighter.

"To thank me for a year of service is what he said."

"He's been married three times."

"I've talked about him too much and you're jealous. Not that—scared. He doesn't even know you exist. Don't worry, darling, I won't leave you."

In a corduroy skirt that matched her brother's robe, tan cardigan, and flats, Ella gripped her bouquet tighter, scurried over, and wrapped an arm around Nick's turkey neck, pressing his head to her bosom. "If what I think is real, is real, and he wants to get me out there with him on the ninth hole, you're coming along."

"Doesn't he already have two grandchildren to care for?"

"So what? He calls the place a palace. Though how he made his money I have not a clue."

"Has he ever touched you?"

"That's private, Nick—well, yesterday as we were closing, he kissed me."

"On the cheek?"

"Lips. I'm late."

"Why are you taking flowers?"

"Why do you think? I cut these from the tubs on the patio before bringing you breakfast."

"Phlox is my passion, Ella."

"I'll plant more."

"Aren't flowers for your boss like carrying coals to Newcastle?"

"Huh?"

"Florals are what he sells." Nick's chin with its scraggly beard dropped. "Tired, Ella."

"I'll help you to bed. Are your pills close by?"

"Oh, yeah. And I was the accountant most likely to become CFO. It all seemed so damned obvious."

▲▲▲

Ella reached John Henry/Flowers in ten minutes. The Land Rover that he'd had repainted silver sat among vehicles left by maybe twenty Walgreens' shoppers. The florist's glass door stood open; bunches of snaps and yellow roses brightened the shelf behind the window. The shop's fragrance made Ella's heart leap.

"For you, John," she told her boss, draped as always in a buttoned vest, houndstooth jacket, and cuffed slacks, hair color matching the Rover's. He limped from behind the counter, getting the hang of an artificial knee.

"For you to take home. From my garden."

"You're late, Ella."

"It's true and I'm sorry." She lowered her eyes, never having seen him scowl. Should she bring up Nick? Doubtful.

"Your tardiness means I'm late for my foursome."

"I didn't know, John. You were coming in afternoons until recently."

"Because I've been wanting to spend more time with you."

"Oh." Her forehead warmed.

"Do you usually come in late?"

"Not at all."

"Behind my back?"

"No!" She thrust the white-blossomed phlox at him.

"Flowers for Christ's sake?"

She watched an artery in his temple swell—gasped as he took the offering, broke the stems in two, and threw the blooms to the concrete.

"I didn't make my bundle selling eighteen-wheelers by arriving late to work. I'll see you at three."

As, stems in hand, he passed, his bulk created a wind. She stayed kneeling on the slab until a woman's voice asked, "Are you okay?"

Today's first customer, slimmer than Ella, had clothed herself in rainbow-striped capris, opened blouse, and orange hat circled by burros of hammered copper.

Gathering up the ruined bouquet—whose broken ends oozed white sap—Ella rose. "Nothing hurts too much."

"I'd like you to help me plan a wedding."

"Yours or..."

The woman flung out a diamond couched in sapphires. "My fifth. Think it's worth the risk?"

Back at You

Though his father taught him to hate birdsong, Chester's ban on neighbors' birdbaths and feeders ends in vehicular disaster.

Abandoned in ninth grade by his mother, who'd died of a ruptured appendix, Chester, a small man, learned to offend no one.

By starting a mustache, for instance, he had offended his opera-loving father, a music-score salesman who lost all his hair after Chester's mother passed. In response to his son's mustache, Chester's father had uncoiled an electric cord and whistled the bird's song from *Siegfried* while bloodying Chester's back.

At age forty-nine, Chester found himself managing a staff of six in the State's Restitution Bureau, charged with securing paybacks from perpetrators of welfare fraud: parents, foster homes, rehab centers, hospitals.

Last year he had bought a townhouse perched on a dirt road north of the Plaza. For a fee he managed the Homeowners Association's half-dozen units. Residents found most of the rules he'd established—no visible trash except on pick-up mornings, stereos silent after nine-thirty—sensible enough. But banning birdbaths, feeders, and suet did cause resentments.

The new owner next to him, retired from the Bronx to spend full time firing ceramic birds, squirrels, chipmunks, and horned toads for sale at Tin-Nee-Ann, Yippee Yi Yo, and other tourist outlets, had agreed to the no-avian-come-ons rule.

A month later she'd broken it, flagrantly. A couple of multideck feeders hanging from poles now flanked a pedestal bath along her drive. Suet and three feeders swung from her rear balcony above two wrought-iron basins.

She'd 'flipped him the bird' when he'd pleaded with her nicely. E-mails from other residents had already let him know they wanted the rule excised. Even Janie Kirsten across the way, a renter he planned to ask out for dinner, had begged him to relent.

But a dozen sessions with a therapist specializing in post-traumatic stress disorder had failed to stop his stomach from cramping whenever he heard birdsong.

Two nights ago an idea had come and yesterday morning Chester had acted, his new neighbor having flown to Hoboken to visit her sister. Now from the huge cottonwood and smaller hawthorns lining his drive shimmied two dozen hip-hop CDs Liquid-Nailed back-to-back. He'd culled them from his collection, drilled holes near the edges, and suspended them with wire to reflect the blinding sun onto his neighbor's feeders. So far they'd worked. No warbling, no whistling.

This Sunday morning he'd brushed finch poop from his porch bench and the retaining wall behind his trees, and driven north to the Windsor Trailhead near Tesuque for his weekly hike.

On his way back, clouds no longer crowded the sun. Chester even found himself humming the Wagnerian bird's warning to *Siegfried*.

Fuck you, Dad, you see? In spite of wasting all that money on therapy, I'm healing.

He steered his convertible up the dirt road past the twenty-miles-per-hour sign he'd had painted. At the top of the hill he veered left, wondering if his neighbor's feeders and bath had stayed vacant.

Across the way, Janie Kirsten, in sundress and straw hat, was kneeling on a pad, planting what looked like violas among her chamisa. Chester called to her. She looked up and waved. Swearing to phone her today, before fixing lunch, he glanced back to maneuver the Saab into his own drive. But glare from the CDs wobbling in the breeze blinded him and the next thing he knew he'd smashed into the trunk of the cottonwood.

He bent over the seat belt groaning and clutched his cramping belly. His temples ached as if burning.

The wrecked car blocked the sun from reflecting off the disks and a flock of finches swooped down, one of them unloading a little poop, like a tear, down Chester's cheek.

Cuddling

Hours after octogenarian Britta takes her beloved terrier for a walk, but loses him to a chipmunk, she prepares kibbles for his dinner, oatmeal for her own, and waits hopelessly.

Every day except weekends the home-care nurse rubbed a topical corticosteroid into Britta's lower leg, applied foam pads, and wrapped them in gauze—trying to reduce the inflammatory arthritis that was giving the eighty-two-year-old's skin the look of red meat.

The itching and burning ebbed as the nurse shut the door behind her. Wrapped in her robe, Britta leaned on her cane and brushed fingers along Oliver's furry cheek. She'd adopted the tan-and-black terrier from Airedale Rescue after learning that its owner had beaten him with a two-by-four to discourage barking. The blows had led to osteoarthritis in both hips.

Oliver and Britta limped into the kitchen where she sponged crumbs from his beard. "You know what, honeybunch? We're going to go get us some fresh air."

It took her fifteen minutes to put on a skirt, blouse, and sweater, and to shoehorn her swollen feet into boots. Oliver licked her hand while she snapped on the leash next to his tag.

They brushed past several bushes fountaining yellow blooms that Britta's husband had planted before a botched hernia surgery ended his life, and were easing up the path between townhouses when Oliver spotted a chipmunk trying to clamber onto a birdfeeder. Britta yanked the leash—but only jamming her cane into the dirt stopped her from toppling. She opened her hand and the dog bounded, listing, toward the rodent now leaping into a juniper. Oliver disappeared after it, trailing the red-handled leash.

Perspiration made Britta's leg feel as though she'd run through nettles. But she managed to hobble home.

No one phoned. She filled Oliver's water dish, wiped his bowl clean, and poured kibbles into it. For her own dinner she fixed some oatmeal, covered it with diced cantaloupe, plunked a bag of stress-relief tea into a mug of hot water, and tucked a napkin into her pajama top. Oliver's scent pervaded the dinette.

She downed two caplets of Prozac for panic and watched Channel 9406's Classic Arts Showcase until nine, when she rose to brush her teeth, swallow Percoset for pain, and leverage herself into bed.

Perhaps tomorrow the neighbor who came Sundays to practice on the baby grand Britta could no longer play would help prepare *LOST DOG* flyers and take them to Kinkos for copying.

Thirty seconds after she'd covered her clock, she heard a scratching at the kitchen door. The sound grew frantic. *You son of a bitch, I'm too old for this.*

Scratch, scratch, scratch...

She struggled into her robe, grabbed her cane, padded across the hall, switched on the light, unlatched the door, and swung it open. Leash end whipping, Oliver pushed her against the jamb. "Bad dog, get down! Bad dog, bad dog, oh, honeybunch, you smell wonderful." She sat and took his head between her hands.

Half an hour later he lay on his side in the living room on the oval throw matted with hair. She set her cane on a cushion, used a sofa arm to help lower herself to the carpeting, and snuggled in behind him spoon-fashion.

Surprise Visitor

Loretta is fed up with lesbian lovemaking, wishing for a way out when a man who vanished long ago reappears.

"**N**o, Loretta, slip the envelopes *into* the cards so that customers can read my stories on the backs. About the kittens and puppies and baby birds I've taken the trouble to photograph. Then slide cards and envelopes into their glassines and place them on the spinner."

Constance's new lover responded by spitting her gum into her palm and sticking it under the counter of the gallery they'd just opened.

Except for nipples large as raspberries, Loretta was flat-chested, with freckle-speckled shoulders and a doe's eyes. Constance had met the girl and her mother at a Friday reception at the Gerald Peters Gallery three months ago where they'd nibbled on rice crackers and talked. Before parting for the Albuquerque Sunport, Loretta's mother had promised to pay six months' rent if Loretta wished trying to sell her abstracts in Santa Fe. The girl had been working on them in the family's attic in Baltimore for two years, following her father's desertion.

"Please let me help, darling," Loretta's mother had said, giving her daughter's ponytail a tug, then throwing an arm as substantial as Constance's around Constance's shoulder. "It's what I always wanted to do, run away. From your father. But he ran first, didn't he?"

▲▲▲

"I'm going outside for a smoke," Loretta told Constance.

"Hold on. Let's see you insert a couple of envelopes right first." Constance fisted her necklace of bronze and coral, longing this bright morning to grab the girl, carry her to the storeroom, throw her onto the couch, and teach her another position, however passive Loretta became when fondled.

The girl faced the white spinner and took the card, envelope, and glassine her lover held out, wondering how come she'd let a woman her mother's age deflower her. Boarding school fantasies had required a man. Plus Constance insisted, before they went at it, on applying a scent under her arms that smelled like bathroom spray.

And how come Loretta had fallen into smoking? Had she grown that edgy, desperate to have customers praise her paintings? Last week she'd splotched with tears the letter to her mother admitting how unhappy she was, adding nothing, however, about Constance's crowding her bed.

The glassine slid from Loretta's fingers and swooped to the floor. Holding card and envelope in her left hand, she stooped to retrieve it but the glassine slipped away and she flung card and envelope after it. "I can't do this!"

"Time to learn, chickee."

Loretta backhanded the spinner. The few cards in its pockets flew out like outsize moths as the rack clattered onto the waxed concrete. The girl wheeled, shook a cigarillo from its pack, marched to the front door, and shouldered it wide.

"Daddy!" she exclaimed, squinting as a cloud drifted off the sun. "What are you doing here?"

Gedankenexperiment

Though Janice has never committed adultery, her now-hospitalized husband has refused to keep fit, unlike the aromatherapist she just shared coffee with in the hospital's cafeteria, who's invited her to his riverside home.

In and out of the emergency room, in and out, and now Janice's husband, Jeff, waited on the second floor for the surgeon to decide—following this afternoon's barium and tomorrow's MRI—if he had to cut to relieve a partial blockage in Jeff's duodenum.

Back home now, Janice flopped exhausted into their living room's tilt-back chair, rested her ankles on the ottoman, and shook off her espadrilles. Her tummy gurgled; she needed to heat frozen lasagna, make a salad. First she'd better think clearly, not to make a phone call she'd regret.

Pretend this Channing *would* like to see her again, as he'd claimed. From her skirt she plucked his card, *Channing Lowe, Aromatherapist.* She sniffed it—nothing, not even the disinfectant with which the hospital reeked.

She and Channing had been sipping coffees in the cafeteria's basement while his wife lay above, recovering from a hysterectomy, three cubicles down from Jeff. Channing had started what lengthened into an hour's talkfest by identifying as ranunculus the blossoms that brightened Janice's blouse.

She bit her upper lip. How often these last few years she had longed to strike up a conversation with such a man—nearer her age, kept himself fit, and yes—like Jeff's brother, the would-be actor—wore a mustache. Her fantasy had led just this far: to experience from a stranger the same tickle Jeff's brother's mustache caused when he flew out from New York for a once-a-year visit.

With Channing, what? He had suggested she drive up to his riverside home to sample his botanical oils, take back vials of grape seed and jojoba to relieve the no-doubt-increasing stress of ministering to her husband.

She wriggled her shoulder blades against the chair's dimpled leather. If she called this Channing—forgive me, God, if You're there—she'd hope to go all the way, feel again the strength of somebody's arms desperate to hold her. She pressed her nipples through her blouse. But the guilt of returning to Jeff fresh from sex with Channing...how many years since her husband had wanted it?

Guilt? Not fulfillment, relief? And, yes, all right, revenge? She propelled herself up, moved barefoot toward the phone, and lifted the receiver.

Her hand started shaking.

Warm the lasagna, open the Parmesan, ornament the lettuce with slices of orange and avocado, end with a scoop—two scoops—of chocolate-mint frozen yogurt. Silence her tummy. Then call.

Down She Goes

Way overweight, Madge has fallen to the ice, but a girl running away and a homeless cripple pause long enough to figure out how to raise her up.

Hip, don't break, Madge begged as she thudded onto a patch of sidewalk ice. The hotel opposite spun topsy-turvy. The polypropylene sack protecting her corrected manuscript—*Why Good Samaritans Give*—skittered against blackened chunks of snow shoveled into the gutter.

Well-cushioned fleshwise, Madge had bundled into a calf-length, quilted coat. Her hip and shoulder ached, though nothing stung except her cheek—cut, she supposed.

Mostly what she felt was mortified, falling right in front of the publisher's steps. The contact lenses she wore for the appointment instead of bifocals seemed not to have dislodged. But close to her nose she smelled blood. So how strange that, helpless but grounded, she felt safe.

She tried to heft her weight onto her elbow, could not. By pushing on her left fist and right forearm, she raised her head a foot, and found herself staring at a twenty-dollar bill captured in the ice.

Laughing hurt. She lay back down. The blinds of the publisher's window were slanted shut. Though he'd asked her to deliver the manuscript before business hours, embarrassment stopped her from crying out.

Cold was beginning to seep through her coat, causing her temples to ache. She watched a pickup full of firewood pass. A hotel van rattled the other way. An Anglo couple who left the hotel arm-in-arm frowned, looking across. No, she wasn't drunk. They hurried toward the O'Keeffe Museum.

A twin-pigtailed girl in yellow-and-blue-striped leggings and hooded jacket appeared from around the corner. She tugged at Madge's hand, but this morning before showering, Madge had weighed herself and pledged once more to join a gym.

The girl scratched an ear. "I can't lift you."

"I know that, darling. Are you headed for school?"

"I'm running away."

"First run to that door and bang on it, will you? My publisher will come out."

"My father's a publisher. I hate publishers."

Heart, whoa, Madge pleaded. "The art director may be in. A woman—can you talk to a woman? You're talking to me. I'll give you twenty dollars."

"Does she look like my mom?"

"I'm sure she does."

"Sorry."

Christ, Madge thought, I'll ice up like that bill.

Just then an Hispanic man in a beige knit cap, long sideburns, a horseshoe beard and soul patch, zigzagged up the sidewalk behind the girl. A bedroll hung roped to the back of his wheelchair. Black tape held one sleeve of his camouflage jacket doubled over half an arm. A scar starting at his jaw disappeared beneath his collar. *Bugger Off* was crocheted into the blanket that draped his knees.

"Move," he growled at the girl and she jumped into a creeping juniper clogged with snow.

By forcing one wheel forward, then crossing his lap with his useful arm to propel the other wheel, he maneuvered the chair beside Madge's head. "Grab my wrist," he said.

"I'm too heavy."

"Grab hold!"

When she had curled her glove around it, he vised her wrist. "Give me a hand," he told the runaway.

With the girl pushing at Madge's armpits, they hauled her to her feet.

"Come back," she shouted, straight-arming the trunk of an apricot bare of leaves. "I want to reward you."

They paid no mind. Madge watched the cripple reach behind to yank the girl's hand off his chair, watched her follow as he zigzagged toward Grant, thrusting a wheel forward, crossing his lap, bearing down on the tire of the other wheel—a man attempting to paddle half a canoe.

First Child

Both of them fat and on edge with her pregnancy, Lisa and Louis seem on the road to divorce—until Valentine's Day arrives.

The Bloomberg Financial News System that Louis had leased was running price/earnings ratios across one of its twin screens when his wife walked into his home office bearing a mug of hot chocolate.

At breakfast he'd ragged her about her new double chin and how thick her ankles were growing.

Louis, I'm pregnant.

And not exercising. Going to be harder to take off once you're free.

Free of our son? Is that how you see it?

Louis dressed every weekday in one of the blue suits he'd bought at Salvation Army. *Suits make me feel grown up,* he'd told Lisa; he'd let the shoulder pads stay.

When they'd met as math majors at the University of New Mexico, he'd been growing a beard and ponytail. He'd rid himself of both three months ago when she'd disclosed she'd missed her period.

He shook his head at the proffered mug.

"Babe, I'm sorry about earlier."

"I've told you not to bother me mornings."

Look who's tubby here, she thought. Flesh tightened the shiny blue gabardine cloaking his upper arms. His ballooning belly matched hers—why she no longer missed making love? "Louis?"

"What?"

"We should both start exercising."

"Huh?"

She slammed the door and spilled chocolate on the rug. She set the mug down, fell into an armchair, and wept. The tears darkened her smock. Both pairs of parents divorced and now this marriage that sucked. A mere two years ago, on their honeymoon, she and Louis had sliced their thumbs and mingled blood in a pact: till-death-us-do-part.

▲▲▲

"Happy Valentine's Day, darling," Lisa tried a week later.

On Louis's mat lay an envelope displaying a crayoned bouquet of tulips.

Nothing lay on hers. From her apron pocket she produced a clear-plastic tub whose top read *Piedras de Chocolate.*

"My favorite!" Louis blurted and opened the valentine with his butter knife.

"You remember the chocolate, anyway," Lisa said.

Five years ago he'd brought to her dorm a larger tub of the cocoa-dusted, caramel-and-milk-chocolate almonds, and refused all twenty, pledging the treats to her.

"Can't eat it," he said now.

"Why not?"

"I started thinking about what you said. Wednesday I bought some weights and Friday squeezed an appointment in with Doctor Radding. Starting today, no sugar for me, carbohydrates, or starch."

"Oh, Louis." She ran close and wrapped his head in her arms. "But I'm fat, too—what'll we do with these?" She brandished the almonds.

"What the hell, mix them in our granola." From inside his shirt he drew out the envelope he'd markered with a neon-red heart.

Decision

While Jocelyn was in Spain hoping to meet a titled lover, her niece, house-sitting, sold off all her furniture and art, and now has disappeared.

Jocelyn, back in August from a month in Barcelona, had asked her longtime friend, Bettie, to join her for a soak at Ten Thousand Waves and then a massage—Jocelyn's treat.

She needed to talk.

"At least you're not trembling now," Bettie said as hot water lapped her fleshy chin.

"Oh, I'm trembling. You just can't see. Because of the jets."

"I feel awful for you," Bettie said.

Underwater, Jocelyn smoothed her palms along her own ribs, hips, and thighs.

"Is there no way to trace your niece?" Bettie asked. "She was so convincing."

"My sister's gone to the cops."

"She must be devastated."

"Before I left for Spain, Donna Quixote in search of a soul mate, sis told me that Meg had developed an obsession for breaking male ranks and becoming a jockey. 'She's never even ridden,' my sister said. 'I sure could use a rest from her pleading for a horse.'

"Perfect timing, I think to myself—and tell sis, 'I'll pay Meg five hundred bucks to sleep in the house and feed the cats while I'm away.' So Meg drives down from Taos that weekend."

"And you pay her half up front."

"Lave me, soothing waters." Jocelyn laid her head back and lowered it until only her face, lined little more than when she'd worked as a model in New York, met the steam.

"How did Meg know where to reach me and other friends?" Bettie asked.

"I keep a box of three-by-fives."

"Which holds...?"

"In Santa Fe maybe a hundred and fifty names."

"The voice mail Meg left me said, 'I'm Jocelyn's niece, a junior in high school, house-sitting while she's gone. I can't find work. Could you possibly drop a ten or twenty through the slot in my aunt's front door? I'd be terribly grateful and I know she would be, too.'

"The chutzpah, Bettie. You've got to admire her chutzpah."

"Nothing compared to what she did next."

"Oh, God, what am I going to do? In two days Carlos flies in from Barcelona for a week. You'll love him, Bettie, a real gentleman. His family lost its fortune in Goyas to the Nazis. Now me without a scrap of furniture. I guess I'll have to pay for his hotel. But I've lost his phone number and Barcelona Information says it's unlisted. Okay, I've started shaking again."

Following her third divorce, Bettie had taken up with a woman, now gone. She threw an ample arm around Jocelyn's shoulders and leaned to kiss a ultraviolet-sanitized cheek. "And I come to your niece's estate sale. So I'll bet do a couple of hundred others because of the ad she placed in *Pasatiempo*. When Meg explained you'd met someone and were prolonging your stay overseas, I bought that armoire you never knew I loved."

"You were only one of maybe a dozen who brought anything back. Who knows who kept what, who's wearing what? Meg probably pulled in fifty grand."

"The cops'll find her, Jocelyn. The FBI? But that beautiful adobe off Canyon must look abandoned. What about all those watercolors? Your wind sculptures?"

"No artworks left, no cats, no chairs, no beds, no sofas, no baby grand, not even patio lounges. Since flying home Saturday I've been sleeping on the air mattress Tom left when I threw him out. Embarrassing, you know?"

"What?"

"Men."

"So you really think this Carlos'll show up?"

Jocelyn shrugged.

"Come live with me. Will you?"

"And turn lesbo?"

"Lots of us do, dear Jocelyn."

Uh-Oh

During the writing-students' discussion about simile and metaphor, Beverly shames her lover, Chad, deciding him in front of the others, to ask Ruth out for dinner.

Like the others at the table, Beverly and Chad had met last summer as low-residency students working towards their Masters in Writing at Vermont College of Fine Arts.

Powerful animal pull from the start...lean and both with brown hair, they exercised at the same gym across from the Veterans National Cemetery.

Two differences: Chad often coughed, though he'd stopped smoking, and Beverly had told him she wanted children.

Currently she lived with her parents on Upper Canyon Road. Chad planned to leave his loft if together they could find an affordable one-bedroom closer to their jobs. He wrote for the *New Mexican*, she acted as admin for the manager of Quinn Stocks & Bonds across the street.

The two older men at the table were novelists. Only Beverly, Chad, and a young woman named Ruth spent their free hours writing poetry, attempting through contests to find a publisher for the manuscript each had spent a year slaving over. Ruth—thickset but with lips, so Chad thought, sexier than Beverly's—served as the group's facilitator Saturday afternoons at Santa Fe's Downtown Subscription coffeehouse.

Today's topic was best ways to use simile and metaphor. Cappucinos sat before the two novelists (not quite yet lovers) while Chad and Ruth had ordered herbal teas, and Beverly her habitual black java.

She swept a palm across her bob and, as usual, led off. "I'm probably the rogue elephant but I say to hell with these—yes, agreed—time-honored devices. Linking disparate images to force an 'aha' creates complications. 'Her dried dugs hung down like bladders lacking wind' was an okay thing for Spenser's *Faërie Queene*, but today we already get too much spin from the media. We should double our efforts—and this includes you two prose guys—to write as simply and truthfully as we can. Her dried dugs hung down, that's plenty, huh?"

"Just so ours don't start to," Nathan said.

Chad started coughing. His chair squeaked and he clapped his napkin to his mouth not to spray tea. "Bev, without metaphor, or that simile you just dredged up, writing's got no flavor. What's the point?"

"I just told you, asshole."

"Bev," Ruth said.

"Well, he loves to put me down."

"That I admit to, chickadee, especially on my Persian carpet after we shower." Though he wished she'd not show off that beautiful bod so flagrantly in public, this afternoon in yellow tee and short-shorts.

"Stop calling me chickadee."

"You seem to like it when we're alone. C'mon." Chad turned his head to cough, then placed his hand against her cheek.

She peeled it away. "I'm telling the group what I think. I have that right."

"You do and I apologize."

"Metaphors and similes," said Nathan, "put me at ease. So much a part of the tradition."

"Metaphor, for me," Ruth said, resting her temples on her fingertips, "is a way to highlight truths that others may not have noticed. Insight, when it works."

"Which it usually doesn't," Beverly said.

"I don't know," Chad said.

"Keep your eyes on me, buster."

"Folksies?" said Ruth. "The idea here's to get along and learn from each other."

"Right on," Chad said. "Take the simile, Happy as a spring shower. Adds mood to mere phenomena, no? Without the linkup, 'happy' and 'spring shower' are threadbare."

"Hey, Chad?" Beverly said. "That's the pathetic fallacy—rain can't feel. Besides, everyone knows what happy is. And we've all been in spring showers. Sometimes you just get drenched. What's so happy?"

"But somehow," Ruth said, "The simile does make me that. I'd like to see 'happy' in a poem. Are you working on one, Chad?"

He stared at her across the table. Not only were her lips bee-stung, but he realized he loved the collegiate way she dressed, this afternoon in a short-sleeved, tan sweater and blue-and-brown, plaid skirt.

He glanced at Beverly, then said to Ruth, "No, but listen, what are you doing for dinner?"

Starting Fresh

Though Dennis promised his dying wife never to date, he plans to break that vow, having bought armfuls of flowers for the shoe saleswoman about to arrive for tea.

Such guilt over so many flowers. Dennis must have spent half an hour at Whole Foods choosing them, plus the French onion multigrain crackers waiting in the refrigerator he thought Emily would enjoy, hummus and lox spread on top.

Items he and his wife had never eaten, so far as he could recall. Nor had they ever set aside an afternoon for tea.

Two years she'd been dead—emphysema. He embraced her pillow every night, promising to obey what she'd begged.

But today he planned to break that vow. Loneliness had become as agonizing as the migraines before his doctor suggested a daily serotonin reuptake inhibitor.

Yes, he lunched with men friends; yes, he wrote lyrics and made up tunes; yes, he handed out sacks of food for No More Hungry Tummies; yes, he took an Hispanic orphan and his sister to the Children's Museum on Thursday mornings.

Loneliness stung as if he walked, stood, sat, rolled, and slept on barbed wire.

Okay, Emily was stout but as cuddly-seeming as his wife had not been. Emily owned Foot S/Mart. In four trips over the past three months he'd bought a pair of boots, a pair of Rockport walkers, and two pairs of slippers. Each time he went in, he saw she'd placed a live bouquet beside the register.

Today a dozen yellow iris waited just inside his front door. Marigolds sprung from a vase on the dining table. The guest bath held more. Red zinnias fountained from a second vase he'd set in front of the living-room's sofa bed. Freezias and what the clerk at Whole Foods had called Spanish bluebells crowded a cut-glass pitcher atop the TV

Emily was due in twenty minutes. Sweat wet his chest and dribbled down his ribs. *I must do this,* he told the memory of his wife. Sitting at the dining table, thighs pressing his hands, he felt as though curled inside a cast-iron pot marinating over flame.

He sprung to his feet, grabbed a bucket from under the sink and pair of shears, ran to the marigolds, snipped their blossoms into the bucket, ran to the TV, snipped off the freesias and bluebells, twisted to face the zinnias, and snapped their blossoms free.

In the guest bath he beheaded more marigolds, stripped off his khakis, Foot S/Mart slippers, white dress shirt, and scrunched down in the tub, pouring the blossoms over his belly and thighs. "I'm sorry, I'm sorry," he cried to his wife.

Out of the tub, he stooped to mash the flowers' reds and oranges and creams and blues into the bucket, hauled on his clothes—and carried bucket, shears, and bathroom vase to the sink in the laundry room, returning to clear the dining and living rooms of containers now filled only with stems.

The bell rang. "Coming," he shouted, shook skinny arms to relax, and sauntered into the hall.

The iris, he'd forgotten to remove the yellow iris. He stretched his lips into a smile and unbolted the door.

Nesting

Aurora, who with her mother's death has begun drinking too much tequila herself, decides this Sunday morning to phone her dad to say she'll be late fixing their usual weekly omelet.

Aurora wished, instead, that she were cradling an armful of jonquils for the boyfriend she didn't have. The stuffed panda, parrot, puppy, bear cub, and burro she carried out of Wal-Mart were for her office. Between the parrot's soft beak and bear's rear end the clerk had tucked a chart from which Aurora hoped to choose new colors for her walls.

Gray clouds spread over the hundred cars parked in the lot. She'd promised her father, wheelchaired with arthritis, to prepare a ham-and-calabacitas omelet for their Sunday brunch. But, oh, in spite of the stack of invoices on her desk waiting to be processed, she longed to drive straight to Sillman, Tapper, Galey, & Ratmore, ascend the stairs she'd been climbing for seventeen years, unlock the pebbled-glass door, and spend the next hour rearranging décor in the corner office the attorneys had given her for Christmas.

By mid-January she'd painted one wall lavender, another pink, the third peach, and the last lemon, hung four tin angels by thread from her ceiling, and taken there—to her father's delight—three teddy bears, the stuffed bulldog, and the rag doll, gifts from her mother that had been perching on a love seat in Aurora's bedroom.

The following day her father had told her to call Habitat for Humanity to get rid of the love seat. And while she was at it, to clear the living room of all furnishings except his and her BarcaLoungers, their side tables, and the floor lamps.

Spring was almost here. The grape hyacinths had started poking out beside the front porch's slab. Would her father next want her to uproot all the flowers her mother had planted? She'd died an alcoholic last year.

Her father's increasing demands to rid the house of everything but basics was driving Aurora to fill her mother's former hidey-holes with her own pints of tequila.

Hoping her bosses would let her repaint her office in Wal-Mart's far bolder colors, she set her bags beside the Oldsmobile's tire and pulled a cell phone from her purse. "Daddy? Listen, we're going to have to enjoy that omelet a little later than I said."

Shame

To seem adult, eighth-grader Aimee wears high heels and unbuttoned blouses, but her teacher shames her to tears for chewing gum.

Aimée's folks had moved from the Mesilla Valley north so that her father could become manager of Santa Fe's Home Depot.

Like her parents, Aimée was tall but no string bean. About to start eighth grade at Capshaw Middle School, she'd developed the breasts of a woman. Embarrassed but proud, and encouraged by her mother—Teen Queen of Las Cruces in 1988—Aimée wore heels everywhere and blouses whose top buttons she left free.

After her inaugral menstrual flow a year ago, she took to chewing gum to stay poised. When she came into her first pre-algebra class in miniskirt and two-inch heels colored to match her lipstick, and sat in back at one of the desks, Mrs. Gonsalves announced, *There will be consequences* for anyone caught chewing gum.

Aimée decided the rule stupid. Gum kept her from smoking, for Christ's sake.

Within a week two Anglos and the Hispanic son of a city councilman, all three shorter than Aimée, had invited her to movies on double dates with friends who could drive. Her parents insisted she decline, told her, *No out-of-wedlock pregnancies*, thank you. Aimèe had smashed her mother's Alpine Dancer with her father's ashtray and stomped from the room.

The next morning she wore blue heels, blue lipstick, a blue organdy blouse, and in the restroom before class dabbed her mother's Kiss of the Dragon on both wrists. She sat in back as usual, chomping on a stick of Juicy Fruit.

Facing the class, Mrs. Gonsalves was chalking an easled blackboard to explain how to resolve a trinomial equation when she stopped, strode to her desk, reached into a drawer, and produced a screwdriver and freezer bag in which she'd folded a paper towel.

Turning heads followed her march between tables until she reached Aimée. "Stand, please," she said.

Aimée gulped her gum and rose.

"Turn your desk upside down."

"Why?"

"You were chewing gum."

"Me? No. See?" Aimée stretched her lips as if yawning.

"You swallowed it."

"This is not fair, Mrs. Gonsalves." She glanced at the three boys staring who'd asked her out. "Where will I put this book and my notebook?"

"In my hands."

Sure she'd begun to perspire, prying free with a tooth what felt like a flake of lipstick, Aimée bent and upended the desk. Dried wads, some old as the desk itself, stuck to its bottom like leeches—albino, gray, speckled, black.

"Yucch."

The class tittered.

"These are for you." Mrs. Gonsalves handed Aimée the screwdriver and bag. "If you can't finish this morning, start again tomorrow."

"This is disgusting!" Aimèe's breasts shook.

"Wow," called a boy to the right.

"You keep quiet, Randall, or you, sir, will be helping."

"Lucky me!"

The class laughed outright.

Aimée's stockinged knees buckled. She crumpled to the floor, fastened the upper button of her blouse, and began to cry, masking her face with her palms.

"Tears will get you exactly nowhere," Mrs. Gonsalves said. "Would you rather we go see the principal to set up a meeting with your parents? We can do that."

"Give me a minute, okay?" Aimée managed. "Just stop talking anymore."

Black Holes

Meg's having sex with the president of her high school's science club causes boyfriend Jason to hurl quotes from Andrew Marvell poems at her.

"You want to know why I took the scholarship to New Mexico Tech?" Meg asked Jason.

"Obvious, isn't it? Anyway, who cares?" He stabbed a bud of broccoli from the heap of stir-fry they'd dubbed the Wonder Lunch, so much energy it gave them.

They'd been meeting at The Wok every Tuesday all summer, trying to reconcile after Meg admitted she'd agreed to a horrible, unfulfilling, guilt-ridden, and miserable fuckfest with the seventeen-year-old president of the science club two months ago.

"I want you and I to be a couple again, Jason."

"With you in Socorro?"

"You could find a job down there."

"Hiding out in the armpit of New Mexico?"

"Armpit? I'll be majoring in physics with an astrophysics option. There's an entire building devoted to this country's National Radio Astronomy Observatory."

"If only you weren't so gorgeous."

"Cut it out, Jason. What about this?" She touched a mole on her jaw. "Plus no arches. And the scar. You know where."

"Your food's getting cold."

She piled a tangle of sprouts and carrots on her fork. "Quit praising my looks, will you? As though that's what matters between us."

He sipped from a cup enameled with cherry blossoms. "I like your fragrance better than the tea's."

"Stop it!"

"'Clora, come view my soul, and tell/ Whether I've contrived it well./ Now all its several lodgings lie/ Composed into one gallery;/ And the arras-hangings, made/ Of various faces, by are laid;/ That, for furniture, you'll find/ Only your picture in my mind.' Bet you don't know the poet."

"Not a clue."

"Andrew Marvell."

"Radio astronomers are romantics, too, you know. They get a much more beautiful picture of our galaxy than optical astronomers can."

"Who cares?"

"Quit saying that! I thought we were trying to keep something going here."

"I'm going home."

"More tea?" Hair drawn into a braid, the Korean waitress lifted the pot.

"Thanks," Meg said.

Jason shook his black curls and grabbed his jacket from a corner of the booth.

"Jason, wait."

"Why?"

"All through high school you'd recite poems to me and I'd tell you things like the Milky Way is fifteen billion years old or planets echoing radar show how far away they are. We loved listening to each other, we *did*. We love hiking together, we love these Wonder Lunches, and we do pretty well in bed, don't we? C'mon, say something. I don't want to lose you, Jason."

"That happened in June."

"A mistake!"

"Something attracted you that couldn't have been the size of his weenie."

"How would you know its size?"

"Showering in the gym. 'Here thou art painted in the dress/ Of an inhuman murderess;/ Examining upon our hearts/ Thy fertile shop of cruel arts.' Waitress? The check?"

"Not yet, Jason!" *Maybe I don't love you but I can learn. Dad's dead, Mom's a vegetable—don't abandon me.*

When the waitress returned, Meg had leapt to the booth's opposite cushion, caught Jason's head, and was forcing her tongue between his soy-sauced lips.

Captain J

"We're heading out of this wacko world," Jeremy, going blind, tells his wife, after accusing her of bedding the electrician.

Lucy and Jeremy had been married forty-three years. But he was going blind and she clung to her church friends because conversations with Jeremy tore her up.

Especially since he'd purchased the rowing machine—aluminum frame, steel legs, steel tension wheel.

He sat on it now in the captain's hat she'd bought at the Army & Navy store, at his request. He wore dark glasses in the dim bedroom, white ducks, and a black tee that read *nmfilmcrew*, though macular degeneration had stopped him from watching even TV for the past nine months. What he called his yachting shoes pressed the machine's footrests as he tugged the cable coiled around the wheel.

Lucy carried up his midmorning snack, squares of fitness bread spread with chunks of sardine. "Time to break, J." Who was going crazy faster, she wondered.

He puffed out air, released the cable's handle, and wiped his forehead with the back of a hand. A clock a foot in diameter perched on the table where Lucy set the platter.

"Sit a moment, dumpling."

He hadn't called her that since the blowup over her weight before leaving Iowa City. Fighting for breath in mile-high Santa Fe, worrying about the drive-by shootings, effluvia from Los Alamos, her husband's eyes and lately his mind, had reduced her to a hundred and twenty pounds.

"Sit why, J?" Though unable to get pregnant, she had loved him once. After he'd retired from Midamerican Energy as a service-line supervisor, they had pulled up stakes to explore New Mexico's wonderland, study its petroglyphs, film its reptiles and birds, videotape changes in its cloudscape. The camper they'd bought then had stayed put on its slab for a year now.

"We're heading out of this wacko world." He felt for the edge of the platter and snatched up a square of bread.

"I don't want to head out, Jeremy."

"Of course you do. You're sick of waiting for me to die and I'm sick of waiting, too. Next Wednesday wear the striped dress I used to see you in. And the turquoise-and-coral earrings.”

“Why Wednesday? I wear those earrings every day. Oh, but all this yakkety-yak is dotty.”

“Reality, dumpling. You thought I'd forgotten? Wednesday a year ago I caught you in bed with Armando, that electrician who installed security lights.”

“So not true!”

“Then how come I wear this copper wire bent around my finger?”

“A wire?”

He straightened his arm. There it was, next to his knuckle, hugging his wedding ring.

“You can hardly see. The cleaning woman twisted that on for you? Now you've got me making the accusations.”

“Wednesday after brushing, plan to pop every pill you've got and I'll do the same.”

Should she call his doctor? Or pretend in two days to follow captain's orders and be free?

Exhaustion

Ginny, a grandmother and married thirty-eight years to Kyle, flabbergasts him by saying she's leaving because she needs to lighten up.

"I don't know what I'd do without you, Gin."

"Let's find out."

"Find out?"

"What you'll do. I'm leaving for two weeks."

"What? Where? When? Why?"

"Let's take 'em in order, Kyle."

"Goddamn it, what is this?"

"A trial separation."

"Why?"

"Your fourth question, and we've covered the first. I'll address 'where.'"

"You can't do this to me, Ginny."

"Male entitlement?"

"I've got to sit."

They took facing chairs at the dining table.

"What's this mean?"

"What, what, what...what's what is that I'm tired of living—"

"Living?"

"With you. Maybe it's those pen protectors."

"My pocket protectors? Why?"

"Right now we're dealing with where. Far from Bert's Burger Bowl, moccasins, Kokopellis, turquoise, tourists, howling coyotes, winters that make my thumbs crack."

"We've been married thirty-eight years!"

"And every day you've stuck one of those plastic pen protectors—"

"Pocket protectors."

"—in your shirt. With three pens."

"In case the others run out."

"Two pens or one pen would break the monotony."

"Of?"

"You, sweetheart."

"I thought you liked to read my stuff."

"Lying for years. How many restaurant reviews can one swallow?"

"I'm supposed to laugh?"

"Do what you like. I've got to lighten up."

"You're sixty-nine, Ginny. We have children, they have children."

"Who rarely call."

"You can't do this!" Kyle hoisted his end of the table and slammed it down. The Santa Clara bowl spun onto the rug, scattering its load of peaches. He bent to grab one and squeezed until the pulp oozed through his fingers. But Ginny was long gone up the stairs to snatch her suitcase from the closet, Subaru Outback sitting ready on the drive.

In Love Again

Aging Erica, feeling madcap with love for Ernie, dumps cottage cheese on her head and dances around the kitchen until best-friend Virginia phones with some pretty upsetting news.

What did Erica care that the spots on the backs of her hands were darkening? Or that she'd brought home a bottle of vegetal-silica capsules to slow the loss of hair? After seven years of walking around shattered, she'd fallen in love again.

Hard, like him. Ernie and she had met as docents at the new History Museum, and yesterday they'd listened to red-winged blackbirds crying *okaleee* at the Leonora Curtin Wetland Preserve while lunching on the chicken-salad sandwiches she'd prepared.

"Okaleee, okaleeeee," Erica sang, whirling on her kitchen's faux-wood floor in a housedress patterned with hollyhocks. She needed to fix breakfast and get down by ten to lead the Musem's first tour. All she wanted to do, however, was dance through the rooms of this hacienda surrounded by piñon/juniper that her husband and she had bought six months before he died of stroke.

To calm herself, she pulled a frosted bag of mixed vegetables from the freezer and pressed it to her neck, then reached into a lower cabinet for a saucepan and frying pan and banged them together. "Okaleee, oh, okaleee."

Ernie loved her, had blurted it yesterday; his cheeks and scalp had turned red. Next weekend he wanted to introduce her to his sister in Tesuque.

Who minded that he was short? Erica capped her hair with the saucepan and waltzed around hugging the frying pan.

Still not enough.

She set the pans on the counter, returned the frozen vegetables, and, hauling a carton of cottage cheese from the refrigerator above, pried off the lid, scooped up a handful, and slopped it onto her tangled pixie cut. The cheese's scent of sour milk smelled to her like strawberry jam. She squirmed as cold gobs ran behind her ears.

Ernie, I must be mad. Now watch this.

She grabbed the container of Pledge from under the sink, screwed off the top, and flung the slippery cleaner in streams across the floor, then lowered herself, knees up, against the cabinet and pushed off, sliding and spinning until she reached the stove. She turned and propelled herself back. Three times, back and forth, whooping.

Her dress was soaked. Cottage cheese had lodged in the hollow of a collarbone. Mad, no question. Erica rested to catch her breath.

The phone jangled next to a jar holding poultry shears and pens. She rose, tugged a dishtowel free to wipe her face, chest, and hair, and lifted the receiver.

It was her best friend, calling from the museum.

"I don't know if I can get there by ten, Virginia."

"Ten fifteen?"

"Maybe."

"Let's start at ten-thirty. Guess who I saw yesterday entering Packards with a woman on his arm?"

Erica's heart jumped. "I don't know."

"Ernie Augustine, I'm afraid."

"He has an older sister," Erica said, and tried to swallow the acid spurting to the base of her tongue.

"If this gal was older, I'd like to know her secret."

"Maybe he has two sisters. A daughter? But yesterday he claimed he was childless. Virginia, no!"

Blood

"War cleans out what's become useless," says Hudson's club-footed father, and when Hudson asks what drugs he's on, raises his cane.

"But, Dad, you've never been in a war. Have you? Your clubfoot..."

Hudson's father, a former book dealer in southwestern military histories, had moved to the Años Dorados retirement complex, following Hudson's mother's death.

Hudson himself had never lived anywhere but Chicago. There, an African American woman helped him run a northside shelter for battered teens.

"You're correct, no baptism of fire." Tom hoisted his black-vinyl-and-titanium-braced foot to the ottoman and sat back. "For you, neither. So what right have you to tell your old man how things are?"

Hudson believed he might retch, so sweetly musty the one-bedroom's living room smelt. How he damned himself for wasting airfare in hopes of a reconciliation. "Stay put, Dad, please."

Tom had reached for his cane.

By June, in the hillside home a mile away, his mother would have had all the windows opened before breakfast.

Hudson rose and with a "You'll have to pardon me, Dad," drew up the shade and cracked the window looking out at the fountain. Almost time for the dinner his father no doubt, again tonight, would not allow him to help fix.

"Pardon you? I've always pardoned you, Hudson. It's touching to have a son forty-one years old who still believes war is wrong. Embarrassing, but touching."

"Why don't we go out, Dad? What was that restaurant you and Mom liked?" A spider bite that Hudson couldn't reach on his shoulder blade began to itch.

"I'd as soon you didn't talk about your mother."

"True, she didn't much value war, either."

"Quit interrupting! Always some smart remark. Your mother was a fine woman, however deluded."

"Tell you what, Dad." Hudson returned to the rattan sofa that had belonged to his mother's parents. "Finish your explanation about war, then I go out and buy us something to eat."

"You have no interest in what I say." Tom drew up his lower lip until it touched his mustache.

"Sure I do."

"I've been studying military history for fifty-five years."

"I know that, Dad."

"This goddamn foot. Now the knee's going." Tom massaged it through his gabardine pant leg.

"You can lean on me."

"In Chicago?"

"You call, I'm here."

"Fat chance."

"Let's hear about war, okay?"

The septuagenarian glared at him before speaking. "War moves civilization forward, turns kingdoms into democracies. We'd not live in this country of opportunity if it hadn't been for wars, starting with the—"

"Revolutionary—"

"Zip it! French and Indian War. The wonder is that the world operates at all. Without the connections civilization provides, the world would stay chaotic. War cleans out what's become useless. In spite of its horrors, no war, no civilization, man's greatest invention. Drugs have their side effects, too."

Hudson filled his lungs, willing himself silent. The claims his father had made for decades still sounded like claptrap.

"What drugs are *you* on, Dad?"

"Huh?"

"Drugs. Prescriptions. For instance, I have to take fluoxetine mornings and half a clonazepam before bedtime to stay balanced."

"Get out, Hud! Go back home to your darky. The medications I require are none of your business."

"You're saying to pack?"

"C'mere."

"Why?"

"I want you closer."

"Why?"

"Blood."

Hudson obediently stood, clomped over in his secondhand boots, and before he could duck, felt the crack of his father's cane against his temple.

Tryout

At seventy-three, Owen's been having impotence problems he's hoping slightly older Lucy can solve, but the fly fishing demo he gives her shatters that illusion.

Two years older at seventy-five, Lucy made Owen feel middle-aged again, ready to resume overnights outdoors. When Owen's wife, avid as himself to fry trout beside a mountain stream, died from an aneurysm in '07, he'd rolled up their doublewide sleeping bag and crammed it with fly rods, propane stove, and Coleman onto the highest shelf in the garage.

Lucy and he had met blazing a trail across land deeded to the Santa Fe Conservation Trust. "I'm a greenhorn at this," she'd told him, "but it sure beats jawboning as a docent to tourists, dumbed down by high-altitude oxygen deprivation."

During the five weeks they'd been seeing movies together and pruning back chamisa, Owen had not summoned the nerve to apologize for his peter's usual refusal to stand tall. Nor had he told Lucy about the guard he wore at night to keep his teeth from grinding. He *had*, however, talked her into today's dry run, practicing casting behind his house, cooking burgers over a burner, spending the night on an air mattress identifying constellations—or making up new ones, why not?

By July, above his seven acres abutting the Santa Fe River, the mosquitoes were dancing aerial ballets.

"My dear," Owen said, standing in boots and hooded jacket beside a Siberian elm, "hold still and close your eyes." When he kissed the back of her neck, strays from her chignon tickled. Planning to undo it once the sun had set, he took a can of repellent from the table and sprayed his face, then squirted hers.

"Jesus, Owen!" The hem of her shirt jerked free from jeans she'd creased that afternoon.

"I thought you saw the can."

"Wrong." She wiped her cheek. "That smells awful."

"I'm sorry."

"Let's go bring out our food before the light fades. Shouldn't we? I'm getting cold."

"What about your casting lesson?"

"Oh, that." She flattened a mosquito probing her forearm.

"I'll find you a sweater."

"No, no, it'll take too long." She folded her arms to her chest as if straitjacketed.

"Grab a rod, then, and watch." He took up his own, having already attached an elk-hair caddis to the end of the line. "Pretend that patch of primrose by the fence is a pond. Stand back, dear; safety first. The wind's building."

She skirted a patch of hairy-leaf kochia to reach the bare ground behind him.

His arm lifted. He locked his wrist and threw the rod forward from ten o'clock to two. The caddis whizzed through the corps of mosquitos, whipping as he fed line from the reel. He cocked his forearm backward to ten o'clock.

"Ah, Jesus!" she cried out.

From habit he brought the rod forward again. The line tightened.

"Stop!"

When he turned she was kneeling, her glasses fallen beside a scrubbed-white sneaker. The fly's barb had embedded in her temple and she clutched her head. Blood trickled down.

"Damned wind," Owen called, running.

"This is what you romantic? Get me into the house."

"You're shivering."

"Of course I'm shivering."

He crouched. Wiggling the hook just drove it deeper.

She ground her teeth.

"I'd better wait till we can turn on some lights."

"Oh, for my life back, before I knew you!"

"You can't mean that, Lucy." He took her elbow.

"Unhand me, sir."

Dark Meat

Edward attacks his mother that she eternally forgets he likes only dark meat when he joins his parents at Thanksgivings, then lies that a broken ankle has stopped his fiancée from coming.

Edward stared at the plate heaped with turkey, squash, dressing, and potatoes just handed him, and lowered his head to his fingertips. "Mother? I'm forty-eight and must have spent twenty holidays with you and Dad, not counting the years trying to grow up, and you know that white meat makes me sick, nauseous, vomit, throw-up. Why, year after year, when I come down to visit, do you serve it to me?"

He raised his head and gazed at the plates she had set on her own mat and his father's. "For you and Dad, dark and white. For me, eternally, one-hundred-percent white."

"Enough said, Ed." His father, freckled dome fringed in gray, strained forward, forked up gobbets of dark meat piled on the platter, grabbed Edward's knife, and shoved meat from the fork onto his son's plate. "And I'll be happy to relieve you of this." He stabbed Edward's white meat and returned it to the platter. "Yes? Start our meal? Agnes, for Christ's sake, stop crying. Ed, thanks very much."

His father moved behind his mother and gripped the sparse-fleshed shoulders she'd draped in an organdy scarf. "Agnes, enough."

"Cast off!"

He let go as though she'd turned incandescent.

"Mother, I'm sorry, I just don't get it."

"I've always wanted the best for you, Eddie."

"I know that."

"May we start now?"

"For you and your sister, the best."

"She's dead, Mother."

"Do you think I'm so addled as to be unaware of that? This evening we give thanks in Melissa's name."

"The food's getting cold, blast it—fair warning." Edward's father mashed dressing on his fork and shoveled it into his mouth.

"Please, Bram, just a minute."

"Too late," his father mumbled and stepped up his chewing.

"Dear Lord, help my husband learn manners, help my son secure steady employment even if not his preference of painting very fine portraits, help Melissa find favor though she terminated her own life after hiring a crook doctor to end the life starting up inside her. And help me, please, Lord, get through another day."

"What a fun Thanksgiving," Edward said, spooned up some squash, and fingered a spear of dark meat to lay on top. "But thank you, Mother, for all the work this took."

"She spent the day slaving."

"While you drank beer watching the game?" Edward asked.

"Always."

"We wondered where you'd run off to, Eddie."

"She could have used a little help, Ed."

"We had understood you'd be bringing along, did you say your fiancée, Eddie?"

"Broke her ankle," he lied. No way he planned to explain that he'd killed the last two hours brooding over lattes at Java Joe's, last week having discovered Julia scrolling through choices on *adultfriendfinder.com.*

Dreamworld

Anita, Burt's wife, had accepted Larry's offer to spend the night, sure—until Burt phoned Larry early the next morning with his own proposal—that they'd fooled her husband completely.

Legs dangling off the mattress this spring morning, Larry was playing with the hair of Burt's wife when the phone rang.

"Larry?"

"You got him."

"Burt."

Burt's wife, Anita, naked and perched close in a chair facing Larry, pushed a mass of her dyed-blonde bouffant up toward him, offering the smile that had persuaded the former hedge-fund manager to suggest she stay the night at his place.

Not a problem. She'd phoned Burt to lie that the Committee for the Museum of Native-American Arts Annual Fund-Raiser planned to work till midnight. She'd also lied that, because of the hour's expected lateness, the Committee had booked rooms at Garrett's Desert Inn. She'd promised to be home in time to fix Burt's lunch today and start the rack of lamb for dinner.

"Burt Uriostegui? Hello." As naked as Anita, Larry closed his eyes to inhale the scent pungent between her breasts from a bout of lovemaking at dawn.

"You know a few other Burts, do you?"

"Well, I..."

"Anita said that you and she and the rest of the committee were holed up at the Desert Inn."

"We worked our asses off, Burt. The truth? I wish I'd never let her talk me into volunteering."

"Do you."

Anita was trying, by scratching two of her silvered nails along Larry's penis, to harden him up again. No luck. He pulled her wrist away.

"Arranging a ball's no fun," he said to Burt, "for a guy who retired early to bone up on fly-fishing." Actually, Larry had stopped managing the Chicago-based hedge fund because his doctor doubted his heart could bear the stress much longer.

"Larry?" Burt asked.

"Yes?" He scooted back against the headboard.

"You felt nothing cold pushed into your left temple about three this morning? I'm assuming correctly?"

"Cold?" Larry glanced at the two empty bottles of Johannisberg Riesling that lay on the carpet.

"Like the barrel of a snub-nosed thirty-eight."

Larry muffled the mouthpiece with his palm and started shaking. His heart began to thud like a pet rat wanting out.

"What's the matter?" Anita shaped the query with lips thin as pencil lines. The wrinkles in her neck rippled. "Babe?" She twisted her chair to press her cheek against Larry's thigh.

"You left the back screen door unlocked," Burt said. "Your place isn't half the size of ours, but, yes, it's gated. Happily I wrote the code down when you had the committee and spouses or whatevers over for dinner last month."

Larry feared anything he'd say would emerge as a croak or squeak. Anita slipped an arm between his sweat-slick butt and the pillow.

"Should have blasted the hell out of you and my own dear whatever, but then I'd have had to off old Burt to avoid the chair. Burt wants to play, too, Larry. I've been eyeing your sister at the museum shop. I favor dark hair though Anita likes hers blonde, claims it blends in better with gray. Is it true what you told me, that the comely Meg has never been with a man? Shall we find out? Anita and I owe you dinner. Bring sis along with you, hey?"

Larry decided he'd better try to protest. "There's no way—"

"Asking you to bring Meg isn't a question, pal. I'll explain the game to our whore when she gets home—she can't afford to lose my family's millions. Remind her she promised rack of lamb tonight, will you?"

The receiver in Tesuque slammed its cradle like a shot. But for Larry the shot was adrenaline. Humphrey Bogart, wronged ex-fund-manager.

"Burt calling? But that's impossible!" Anita's voice had turned husky, a dead ringer for Lauren Bacall's.

Larry stroked her hair, smoothing it along her shoulders and sagging breasts. "You and me, kid."

"Kid? You've never called me that before. Thank you, darling." She sat up straight. "Was that really my husband?"

"We're going to beat this rap," Larry said.

Testing

Peggy, subject to psychosomatic cramps, flirts with her psychophysiologist to talk him into letting her answer the MMPI test's five-hundred-plus questions out of doors, where she'll feel less pressure.

"The five hundred and sixty-four questions on the Minnesota Multiphasic Personality Inventory will keep you in this little room for perhaps two hours, Peggy. There's a kettle of water on the hot plate, tea bags and freeze-dried on the shelf. No window, I'm sorry."

"What if I cramp and have to…"

"The bathroom's through that door. But relax. As I've promised, the MMPI is going to help us figure out why your gut brain is causing your colon to spasm. And figure it out we will, with these weekly get-togethers and probably a couple of meds. What we need is patience."

Clyde Remmington, PhD, who specialized in psychophysiologic disorders of the abdomen, stood in the hallway in a persimmon-hued shirt and green tie. Arrived from London twenty years ago, he wore his hair slicked back and parted in the middle. The frames of his glasses were as black and shiny as his hair.

This morning Peggy, a social worker recently divorced—whose son had not spoken to her in the three years since leaving college—had slipped into a sunflowered sundress and red sandals, hoping that protective coloration would hide the dread she felt. On the way to the therapist's quarters, she'd stopped for a muffin at Chocolate Maven, then realized she'd be late and stuffed it into her handbag.

Dr. Remmington had told her he'd become like a mole, carrying his lunch to a small office fridge mornings, remaining at his desk until quitting time. Grateful for his calm, she had moved to hug him but he'd raised his hands no. Code of ethics.

Now he reached to switch on the room's fluorescent. "Remember not to think too much, just fill in each bubble whose statement seems truest at the moment. Thinking brings trouble."

She lowered herself to the steel-framed chair. "Dr. R? You're not going to like this, and no doubt it breaks all the rules, and I know might even screw up the results, plus no one's probably ever asked—"

"What is it?"

"The idea of your shutting the door on me for two hours creeps—"

"I'll look in if you like."

"Why can't I carry the test and a clipboard up into the park?"

"Absolutely not."

"Fresh air, Dr. R."

"I'm sorry, Peggy."

"Sunshine. Birdsong. I can breathe. And swear not to think."

He curbed his chuckle. "You won't be able to concentrate with the traffic."

"It's only nine o'clock Saturday morning! And the park is tucked away."

"This testing is costing you three hundred dollars. Your insurance won't cover it."

"I'll take it again if my answers seem gobbledygook."

"Gobbledygook."

"At least I got you to smile."

"You're prepared to throw away three hundred dollars?"

Suppose he was right? He'd been at this work for over thirty years.

"I can be more honest up there. And I bet quicker."

She jerked forward; her colon had twisted.

"Pain?"

"Bearable."

"You're serious about going topside?"

"I think so."

"No thinking."

Both laughed.

"I can't let you do it, Peggy. I need to keep you near me."

Well, hearing that felt good.

She winced at the stab in her gut, caught her breath, and asked, "Will you share my muffin later? Assuming I can finish."

"What flavor?"

"Pumpkin."

"Deal," he said and extended his hand.

Breakout

On a hike, Danny breaks through brush to face a pistol wielded by the runaway sister of a millionaire who's been raping the niece cowering beside her.

Danny, a student at St. John's College, dearly wished he'd worn leg warmers. He was hiking about four up an arroyo reddened by willows, between the college and bluff opposite that held faux-adobe mansions of maybe a half dozen multimillionaires.

He looked for a blind behind which to pee, and clambered up between boulders and across bark-beetle-felled branches toward a thicket of piñon/juniper. Chickadees fled his approach and puffs of rabbitbrush clung to his red fleece. When he reached the thicket, he turned sideways to wedge through, unzippering as he did—and when he could face forward again, found himself looking upslope into the barrel of a tiny, tortoiseshell-handled pistol.

The woman stood beside a pigtailed girl in front of a pup tent camouflaged black and green. She wore a sweaterdress the same red as Danny's jacket and a belt of silver conchos. What looked like a wedding ring hung on a chain around her neck. She'd swept black hair into a French roll; a couple of sheaves had shaken free.

Danny glanced at her face, pocked but made perfect under heavy powder. Her perfume sweetened the turpentine scent of the piñons.

He sneezed.

She shoved the girl behind her and dropped penciled brows. "Who are you? Did he send you?"

"He?"

"My brother. We live on the bluff." She jerked a thumb up past her shoulder.

"No one sent me. I was hiking. I had to take a leak."

"Raise your hands—never mind. You don't look like the kind of friend he'd have."

The girl peeped from behind the woman as Danny managed to zip closed.

A gust made him shudder. "What's with the tent?" He glimpsed a pair of sleeping bags inside, rumpled on top of air mattresses laid on a patch of level ground.

The woman lowered her gun. "Will you stand guard? And tonight, sleep in my bag with me?"

Another rich, Eastside crazy, Danny thought.

"Did you hear that branch crack? He's heading down!"

"I heard nothing, ma'am."

"Take her with you, quick."

"What?"

"He'll force her to make love with him again."

The girl ran to Danny and stuck a small hand in his jeans' pocket.

"Is that your mother?"

"My father's sister."

"Holy shit."

"She won't stay on her meds."

"He *is* coming—you hear the leaves crunching? He goes dark or I go or we go dark together," the girl's aunt said.

A whole nest of nutcases...though Danny now thought he did hear crackling. He wrested the girl's hand free and pushed her toward the woman.

She flicked the pistol's barrel at him like a whip. "Take her or you're dead meat, nice boy."

The girl tugged him into the thicket.

By the time both emerged on the slope's downside, his wrists and face stung with scratches and his tongue's tip tasted blood.

"I've got to pee," he blurted as behind them came what sounded like a firecracker; another. Then the girl screaming beside him.

Taking Over

All just-retired Louanne wants to do is work her chisels and lathe, but first she has to convince her grieving, vastly overweight mother that the latter's no longer the household's boss.

All Louanne longed to do, retired at last as the supermarket's general merchandise manager, was to work her lathe and chisels again, turn out bowls to sell at Jackalope and maybe Saturday mornings at the Farmer's Market.

But the only space for a shop was beneath her mother's bedroom, and Ruth—her mother, who owned the home—laid down the rules.

"Your marriage went three years childless and you're back, fine and dandy. Right here for more'n a year I tried to save your sister. You know I did. But crack won. No more attempts at salvation for this sinner. You sleep when I sleep, eat when I eat, pay rent like she did, and the rest of the time jist plan to keep me company."

After her mother had finished decreeing, she snorted into a tissue. Louanne understood: Beth had been her mother's favorite.

Grown to two hundred and forty pounds since Beth's death, Ruth now spent every day watching talk shows and news, reality shows till nine at night, talk shows again till one. Each day she polished off two family-size bags of chips. When she slept she became a chainsaw ripping apart the wall between her and Louanne's bedrooms.

Before the court had ordered Louanne and her husband to sell their house, she'd grown used to turning bowls before leaving for work. But her mother snapped that early-morning commotion 'down under' would wake her way before ten.

Louanne was about to call her doctor to plead for doubling her dose of Klonopin when an idea struck. Long ago her mother had liked to take the girls camping.

▲▲▲

Mother and daughter munched on sugar-free wafers thirty-five miles east of Santa Fe. Rocks ringed an after-dinner campfire beside the used, tow-along camper Louanne had managed to afford. Their sleeping bags lay on bedrolls near Louanne's Chevy—she planned to clamp on earmuffs when her mother started snoring.

A webbed chair held Ruth's bulk. Louanne sat cross-legged on pine needles in leather shorts. She locked fingers against the back of her head, close-cropped since the divorce, and stared at the stars. "We do get our snorts and giggles, don't we, Mom? Waking to birdsong and all this fresh air?"

"I miss my TV, Louanne."

"Sure, and me my bowls."

Maybe her mother liked wolfing down chips and adding weight, mourning Beth's absence until her heart gave out. Louanne, however, as the leftover sister, did not wish to watch. "We're got places to go and people to see," she said.

"Like jist who?"

"Like your chum from high school you contacted in Denver."

"We could call her and explain."

"Like Don Rattleson up in Montana."

Ruth wiped her nose. "He won't even know me."

"He's expecting us, Mom."

"I'm embarrassed." She pulled out the sides of her dress to emphasize how she'd grown.

"You promised when we hit the road I could set the rules, recall that?"

Ruth rubbed her neck and stared at her daughter through puffed eyes. "Yeah, okay, honey. Okay."

Sleight

Though Joseph, hoping to find a young live-in, has committed his wife to an assisted-living facility, he breaks into tears watching her perform magic tricks for money at the mall.

The mall opened officially at ten. Capped in a Tam o' Shanter with pompom on top, Audrey stood alone in the corridor between the bridal shop and gun dealer, practicing, her husband, Joseph, supposed, a trick she'd said she'd seen on TV before he'd phoned yesterday.

She threw her arm out of a cotton jacket's sleeve as though casting with a fly rod, nudged smudged glasses up the bridge of her nose, and threw out her arm again.

"What are you staring at? Are you waiting for me to drop dead?"

"I'm waiting to take you home," Joseph said.

"You're not waiting to take me home. You're waiting to hustle me back to the group."

"Where is the group, Audrey?"

"At Starbucks of course. Go away. You're cramping my style, sir. Shoo."

Still lithe at eighty-one, Audrey flung the back of a hand laced in veins at her husband, and scampered in white-leather shoes down the corridor. She disappeared around the corner where the jeweler was setting out rings.

When, last year, medications couldn't stop Audrey from placing her wristwatch in the freezer at night to increase a day's longevity, from fastening her brassiere over her blouse, from insisting that waiters squirt a dab on their hands of the sanitizer she took from her purse, and from patting mouthwash between her breasts and behind her ears before meeting friends, Joseph and their doctor decided Audrey required professional care.

Mi Casa offered assisted living at a cost that Joseph, who sold works of Santa Fe sculptors over the Internet, thought he could afford. Not a prayer, however, that he'd move in with her. Because of his snoring, they'd chosen to sleep apart, upstairs and down, when they'd bought the condo near the Plaza five years ago in which to live out old age. His dream now was to find a younger woman to cook and clean, offering her Audrey's bedroom and bath rent-free.

In the cowboy boots that made him feel virile, he followed his wife around the corner to see maybe a dozen people waiting for the manager of Ross Dress for Less to roll up the steel security curtain. Most of the crowd was watching Audrey. Joseph walked closer to see her cast her arm all the way down. A quarter slid from her jacket's sleeve to clink on the buffed concrete.

"Thank you, ma'am," she called, picked up the coin, and shook the hand of a Hispanic woman who stood open-mouthed. "Anyone else wish to contribute?" Audrey dangled her Tam o' Shanter upside down. "I need a cup of black java to get me back to the shelter. Thank you, sir." A tall, mustachioed Anglo in a buttoned sweater handed her a dollar. Audrey stuffed the bill into her skirt pocket, recapped her head, pulled at her jacket's collar, and hid the quarter underneath, atop her shoulder. She threw her arm down and the coin clinked on the floor. "Thank you, miss," Audrey said to the girl clutching the Hispanic woman's dress. "Anyone else, please? I need just a cup of—"

"Excuse me," Joseph said, pushing forward. He gripped Audrey's elbow. "Come on to Starbuck's, come along."

She shook free and said loudly, "He loves me, you know, even though he wants me gone. All he has to do is stay away. But he can't, he misses me desperately. He watches out for me. Joseph, beloved, you must let me be. Look at the crowd I've drawn."

Joseph did look at the women and men, Hispanic, Anglo, two Native Americans, a child cradling a puppy, a couple of white-turbaned Sufis—and felt tears cooling his cheeks. He realized he hadn't cried since committing her, and backed away, turning to seek out whoever at Mi Casa drove residents on Saturdays to the mall for muffins.

Exercise

Now that Penny has moved in with older, investment-guru Nevil, they need to learn how to share his exercise room—or do they?

On Sunday afternoons, Nevil used the den downstairs to catch up by phone with his daughter and grandchildren in Chicago. This allowed Penny to use, undisturbed, the master bedroom upstairs for her practice. Carpeted in orientals, it was twice as large as that in the apartment she'd broken the lease on to move in with Nevil. They'd met while searching for birds with fellow Auduboners. But already she half-missed returning from the field to solitude.

Penny had shut the wooden slats in the bedroom's bank of windows. She was sitting on her heels, butt resting on the stool she'd pulled from beside Nevil's armless stepper, when she heard moccasins slapping the stairway's tiles.

He opened the door and brushed a palm over wisps of blond hair. "Grace hung up on me. She claims that since you moved in, I've become too controlling. Mind meditating in the bathroom or down in the guest room? I think I should work out."

She did mind, yes, go away. But shut her eyes instead of speaking.

"Do you think I'm too controlling?"

"You're scared is all, Nevil. That my moving in will split us up." She kept her hands spread on her sweats. "We're both scared. I do relish my hour alone in this room you've decorated so beautifully."

"Paid for through the nose. To please a young bird. Why don't we try sharing?" He drew the slats to the top of the window facing the entryway's aspens, returned to the wall, hoisted the stepper's conglomeration of pistons and treads, and carried it to a spot on the carpet facing the dresser he'd bought her.

He shuffled out of his moccasins, climbed up barefoot, and began to stomp. "You should be doing more of this kind of thing, chicken."

"My practice keeps me fit."

"No aerobics in it. I worry." He shoved his elbows back past his ribs, left elbow with left foot, right elbow with right foot. "Look at those aspens' yellow leaves. Like coins clicking against that sky. I should be a poet, no? Instead of some aging investment guy."

"I'll go use the guest room," she said to his back.

He whooshed out breath, climbed down, reached for a neoprene mat, and unrolled it. "We need to learn to each do our own thing together."

Flipping her ponytail across her shoulder, Penny grasped a leg of the stool and stood.

"C'mon, stay. I keep hearing Grace slam that damn phone down." He gazed at Penny through rimless glasses. "I'll make the room dark again."

"No huffing or puffing."

He laughed, lowered the window's slats, then lowered himself to begin a dozen push-ups.

She replaced her butt on the stool, took in through her nose as much breath as she could, held it, and let it slide free.

Nevil tried hard not to grunt, failed. He rose from the mat in hope that none of his joints would creak, and placed his feet again on the treads. He pushed down and began to throw back his elbows, forcing his thighs to thrust faster.

Penny was trying to still her monkey mind, stop its self-gratulation that Nevil's panting had become mere autumn wind, when she heard a cry and thump. She twisted to spot his glasses under the dresser and Nevil on the rug, squeezing his left bicep and groaning.

Busy

About to pass out on mescal martinis, Barry hopes the phone's ring means the woman whose trees he trimmed this morning wants him in her bed tonight, but it's his sister with news that their father has died.

Helped by a four-year scholarship, Barry's parents had sent him to Harvard to launch a career as a lawyer or physician, his choice. Or return to Los Angeles to move up in his father's paint-manufacturing business.

Most important were the lifelong friendships Barry would start, his father had emphasized. "Wish I had your future, son." Smack on the back from the man whose rages used to drive Barry under the bed.

So how come seven years later Barry found himself making ends meet by pruning trees in Santa Fe? Living by himself in a slapdash afterthought conceived by the owner of Shannan-Orrin Gallery as storage for her not-yet-displayed paintings, renting out the shack's second bedroom.

The big adobe where she lived with her girlfriend blocked Barry's view of the Sangres. All he could see from the kitchenette where he now sat were trash cans.

He listened to the raindrops splash in the bucket he'd set in what she sardonically called the great room, and polished off a second Mexican martini, his invention that substituted mescal for gin. He gulped the olive down, refilled the stemmed glass, drizzled in vermouth, and plopped in another olive from the jar. The thought of preparing salad and heating the frozen enchiladas he'd planned for dinner made him nauseous.

The phone rang. Hey! Probably the woman in Wilderness Gate who'd greeted him in her robe, whose ponderosas he'd trimmed this morning. Not that bad a looker. He rose with his drink and pulled the receiver off its wall cradle.

"*Hello* there."

"It's Andrea, Barry."

"Oh."

"You don't seem exactly thrilled to hear my voice," said his sister. Andrea lived northeast of Los Angeles with her husband, Clay, and four children.

"I'm busy."

"Doing what?"

"Planning my future."

"Bad news, Barry. Dad died last night."

He drained his glass. "That's bad?"

"He fell downstairs."

"*You* don't seem too shook up."

"Clay had a hard time working with him as heir apparent. Dad always figured you'd come to your senses."

"Clay must be thrilled."

"I just can't talk to you anymore."

"Then don't."

"What's happened to us, Barry?"

"The usual."

"The funeral's Saturday. Mom wants you here. Will you come?"

"I'll have to consult my calendar." He stared at the half-drained bottle of mescal. "Right now I'm in kind of a hurry."

The click at the other end sounded like a rifle's report. Barry tried to replace the receiver but missed. It bounced off the wall and plummeted on its cord.

Suppose the aging honeypot in Wilderness Gate had been trying to reach him while he and his sister talked? He held the receiver to his ear. Beep, beep, beep, beep ...yes! But what if she hadn't left her phone number? Wait, he'd scribbled it on a scrap. In his pocket? Yep. He poured his glass full, slid down the wall to the linoleum, and punched in the password to reach voice mail.

Dastard

Though Fidelity has decided to dump staid fiancé Bob for a poet she met over spilled wheat germ and slept with that night, she experiences doubts when the poet laughs off her mother's rage.

"I still feel guilty," Felicity said, rolling toward Rich and kissing his lips, his near cheek, his forehead, his chin—snuggling her face between his shoulder and neck, then flinging herself to her back and pulling the covers up. "And hooked."

"Hooked?" He shut his eyes against the Sunday morning light muscling into his walk-up. It brightened the clothes Rich and Felicity had thrown last night on the oriental rug his mother had left him. Its dark blue matched the ceiling and dresser a former girlfriend had painted.

"Hooked on you."

"I love you, Felicity. My life's been recharged." Convinced, he scrambled onto his hip to more comfortably explore her breasts, belly, and below. "Both our lives recharged, now that Bob's bopped out of yours."

His palm relaxed on her pelvis.

"He screamed at me Thursday when I returned his diamond—he wept, Rich, threw himself into a fetal position across the bed his folks let me spend overnight in, once I wore his ring. We'd planned to live with them until—"

"You've told me about it." How weary he was of hearing what Bob's mother did, what Bob's father did, what Bob did, said.

"I just couldn't make love with him anymore, Rich. Once I'd met you."

"These things happen, pumpkin."

"I love 'pumpkin.' Will you call me it always?"

"For as long as we're together," He raised his head and kissed her. "Are you starving?"

"I want to talk some more, okay? This has happened so fast. Meeting you...a week ago! Doesn't it seem unreal?"

"Not to me.

"But literally bumping into each other, my dropping the wheat germ, your helping the clerk clean up, suggesting coffee, learning we're both serious poets—that we grew up in Cincinnati. I mean, c'mon, Richard. Unreal."

She rolled over to face him.

"What's unreal for me is Bob. In two months you were going to marry a guy who sells life insurance?"

"Life and liability and home and auto. Totally nice guy. His father owns the agency."

"Your security blanket."

"Sure. *You* get by on an inheritance. My mother's in her late sixties and still has to show up at the dress shop. Now I'll have to keep my job, too."

"We're going to live on what I get a month." Rich had recently changed his mother's blue chips into high-yield bonds. So far so good.

"You really think we can, Rich?"

"Absolutely."

"Rich?"

"Yeah?"

"My mother has written you a letter."

"What for?"

"It's in my purse."

"Do I want to read it?"

"I'd just as soon you didn't."

"Then tell her to stick it—"

"Richard!" Felicity sucked air like a caught fish. She sat up against the pillow and pulled the covers to her collarbone as strands of her long hair striped her face.

"What's her problem? She thinks I can't support you? She's never even met me."

"She calls you a dastard."

"A dastard? What kind of strange person says that?"

"She says it four times."

"Well..." Rich leapt from bed and threw out his hands. "Your mother's antediluvian and uninformed." A sudden need to pee propelled him around their heaped clothes.

"Oh, my God, Bob's folks," Felicity moaned, wrapping the covers around her neck. "What have I done?"

Rapt

Gray-pigtailed poet Chastity Burns holds a post-stroke reading in a friend's apple orchard, and though she collapses, nothing can stop her recitation.

Nine friends gathered near the Santa Fe River in a grove of apples to hear Chastity Burns read from her latest collection, published by a press in Tallahassee no one had heard of. Just recovered from a stroke, Chastity had self-published two previous collections of poetry. So this was not only a comeback party but a nice-going-finding-a-publisher party, too.

She looked blithe in her flounced skirt and nasturtium-flowered blouse. Her husband and barrel-chested son had carried folding chairs through the horsetails down from our hostess Marian's home, a refurbished carriage stop on the old El Camino Real leading south to Albuquerque.

The lectern stood in weeds beside card tables laden with what we'd all brought: Brie and jack cheese, crackers, strawberries, cherries, wedges of pineapple tart.

The afternoon swarmed with bugs. Marian was talking to Bruce Orf and me when she started winking and moving her jaw as though trying to return the bone to its sockets—then turned and spit out a mosquito.

She strode to the lectern, urging everyone to move their chairs into the best shade. "I do love to talk but, you'll be happy, not today. Chastity, welcome back. We applaud your most recent accomplishment." Marian began to clap, as did we.

Rising, Chastity smoothed her fist down a long, gray pigtail. "You are my family but some of you won't agree with what's in my latest." Her voice had grown huskier since the stroke. She swept her arm in an arc and picked up *Roaming Around the Backwoods of Love.* "More truth-telling in this third collection—less love of nature, life is hunky-dory. Let's try this short one called 'Lust.'

"'Curling, purpling, thrusting an emergent/flower that lifts day-to-day petals/like loin cloths, revealing the genitalia:/swollen banana fingers capped with cream,/dropping nectar of which small finches sing,/shocking abandon of fertile and phallic bloom.'"

Polite applause, a few hmms, a couple of huhs. I glanced at Chastity's husband, Herb, shrunken next to their son Clyde, who sat staring toward the river. Herb, pinched face dappled, caught me looking. One side of his mouth stretched under a whitening handlebar.

"This next is dedicated to my husband and boy, who, well, kept me sane when I couldn't meet with my writing group. My writing group," she repeated. "Couldn't at all, lay in bed counting cracks in the ceiling. The poem's called 'Thanks.'

"'Herbie and Clyde, you earthbound angels, backwoods bred,/bringing me slurpies and turkey bacon, making eyes at this old hag/hanging in there for who-knows-why/when the fingers can't curl, the left eye close,/the nose twitch. Why hanging?/Because, you sweet alyssums, you're—'" Chastity paused, frowned, finished up. "'Because you're there.'"

A beetle had alighted on her forehead. She merely nodded and ran her fist down her pigtail. "I can curl my fingers now, I can twitch my nose." She demonstrated and we clapped.

"Now let's try something different, something try. 'Reinventing Reincarnation.'" She closed her eyes a moment, snapped them open, drank limeade from the glass Marian had placed on the lectern's shelf. "'Reinventing Reincarnation.'

"'Dear God wherever, I don't want to come/again, even as a leaf of grass—'" she struck her neck and I could see the mosquito splatter as the beetle on her forehead whirred off. "'Cradle me memory,/cradle your darling daughter,/as if—'" She stopped, peered at the page. "'As if a devil groaned, hooves of dark, a dark—bull/clubbed and torn,/hail goddess'—oh, God."

Her fist thumped her left breast and she collapsed behind the lectern. Herb and Clyde, billed caps on backwards, leapt up.

A moment later Herb got off his knees. "She'll be all right, folks. She's whispering the rest of her poem. Anyone got a cell? Does anybody know first aid? "

▲▲▲

Bruce and I came to visit a couple of weeks after Chastity left Intensive Care. She knew us fine but when we asked when she hoped to get back in the swim, she answered, I think, "Beauty bested.'" And began to recite what sounded like a poem penned in a private language.